DEAR LOYALTY

KT-164-511

DEAR LOYALTY

Denise Robins

KIRKLEES CULTURE AND
LEISURE SERVICES

ACC NO.	351 575 869
CLASS NO.	
Order No.	
Date	
Price	
Supplier	
Loc.	

CHIVERS
THORNDIKE

This Large Print book is published by BBC Audiobooks Ltd, Bath, England and by Thorndike Press®, Waterville, Maine, USA.

Published in 2005 in the U.K. by arrangement with the Author's Estate.

Published in 2005 in the U.S. by arrangement with Claire Lorrimer.

U.K. Hardcover   ISBN 1–4056–3192–9 (Chivers Large Print)
U.K. Softcover   ISBN 1–4056–3193–7 (Camden Large Print)
U.S. Softcover   ISBN 0–7862–7227–9 (General)

Copyright © 1993 by Denise Robins

The moral rights of the author have been asserted.

All rights reserved.

All situations in this publication are fictitious and any resemblance to living persons is purely coincidental.

The text of this Large Print edition is unabridged.
Other aspects of the book may vary from the original edition.

Set in 16 pt. New Times Roman.

Printed in Great Britain on acid-free paper.

British Library Cataloguing in Publication Data available

Library of Congress Cataloging-in-Publication Data

Robins, Denise, 1897–
    Dear Loyalty / Denise Robins.
       p.   cm.
    ISBN 0–7862–7227–9 (lg. print : sc : alk. paper)
    1. Triangles (Interpersonal relations)—Fiction. 2. Petroleum industry and trade—Fiction. 3. Inheritance and succession—Fiction. 4. Conflict of generations—Fiction. 5. Alexandria (Egypt)—Fiction. 6. Secretaries—Fiction. 7. Large type books. I. Title.

PR6035.O554D43 2005
823'.912—dc22   2004061741

I

The sun beat down pitilessly upon the desert. Lucie Bryant sat on the running-board of her car and looked through her dark glasses at the far horizon, her face a study in despair.

For the last three hours she had sat here like this staring at space, or walked up and down, around the car, realising, with that most hopeless of all sensations, that she was lost. Lost in the desert, and yet she could not be twenty miles out of Cairo.

She knew now that she had been a fool to come. Somebody had told her that only cars with big desert-tyres, especially constructed for the soft sand, should venture off the beaten track. She had been foolhardy—ridiculous— and this was her punishment. For a considerable way the little car had stood up nobly to being bumped about on the rough surface, which was a mixture of sand and stone, and here and there a tuft of green, but finally it stuck. Stuck and refused to move. And three hours ago Lucie had tried walking, then given it up as an impossibility. She must keep the car in sight, and beyond it she could see no road. She might walk for miles and find herself going deeper into the wilderness.

Lucie had always loved the desert. She had longed to come out here and be alone, as one

1

could never be alone in the city of Cairo. She had wanted to forget work, and to dream her dreams undisturbed. One could be alone and dream in the desert. It was beautiful and inspiring. Just these miles of undulating sand, golden in the golden sunlight, under a sky of dazzling blue.

But to be lost like this was another thing. Glamour was still here, in these infinite wastes. The sheer beauty of the scene still clutched at her heart and captured her imagination. But she was lost. And she was afraid. For she knew her Egypt and this was only February. As soon as the sun set it would grow bitterly cold. Even though it was hot enough now to sit without a coat.

Surely somebody would come along? A caravan . . . camels . . . an Army lorry . . . anything! Surely she could not just go on sitting here alone for days and nights until she starved!

Lucie was not a coward, but her heart quailed at that last idea. Yet how easily she had driven here! How could she have dreamed that it would be so difficult to retrace the way. At first she thought she could follow the tracks of her car. But she had lost them and taken the wrong route once or twice. There had been other cars here as well as hers. That at least gave her hope that there might be yet another before nightfall, and that she would be rescued.

2

She lit the last cigarette in her case, sat smoking it, thinking how delicious a cup of tea would be . . . a drink of any kind! And what a difference it would make to hear a human voice or see a human being. An unusual ambition for Lucie who, after working all day in an office amongst people, appreciated being alone.

A little while ago she had watched a long line of camels on the horizon moving slowly northwards. Useless even to try to get to them. Long before she could reach them, they would be gone. But she had watched the silhouettes of the animals until they had disappeared into the shimmering distance. And even in the midst of her plight, thought what a lovely sight they made.

She tried not to let fear occupy her mind. She concentrated on the thought of her existence in Cairo, her work, her friends. She was personal secretary to Edgar Lorrimer of the Near-East Petroleum Company. It was a job she had held for the last two years, since the death of her father, who had been an engineer, in Alexandria. She wondered, wryly, what her employer would say if she failed to turn up in the morning. But no! she couldn't be here all night, she *couldn't* be!

Restlessly she got up and began to walk round and round the car. Poor silly little Morris, sticking there in the sand, refusing to budge. And what an idiot she had been to disregard all warnings, and come out here like this alone.

It was very still in the desert. She could hear nothing but the faint yapping of pie-dogs . . . those lonely, miserable scavengers of the East. Somewhere . . . she knew not in which direction . . . lay the white buildings, the minarets and mosques of Cairo. And somewhere, at this hour, perhaps Crash Lorrimer was playing polo. Crash . . . handsome, irresponsible young man . . . her employer's only son. That was the name they had given him in the Regiment a year ago, when he had first joined it. '*A young devil*' his father called him. '*The hell of a lad*' said his brother-officers. '*Too gorgeous for words*' from the women. All those women, old or young, came out to Cairo for 'The Season' and vied with each other for the pleasure of being taken out in Crash Lorrimer's racing-car.

Sitting here alone with her thoughts, Lucie admitted to herself that she had adored Crash for a very long time, and that adoration was about as hopeless as her chances of being found here in the desert tonight. But she liked to picture Crash on his polo pony; Crash, grandest of riders, galloping superbly over the polo-ground in the Sporting Club at Gezira. How far was that from here? If only she knew! She thought desperately about him in this hour, while she walked up and down, her feet sinking a little in the soft sand.

4

What would Crash say if he heard in days to come that she had been found here, a poor little corpse, victim of hunger and thirst? Nothing much, she told herself, trying to keep her sense of humour. Only that she had been a fool. He wouldn't be very sorry. He cared nothing for his father's secretary. Whenever he came into the office, he was always charming to her. But then Crash was charming to all women. And one in particular. That fair-haired 'playgirl', Amanda Portlake, whom Lucie had once heard Crash, himself, describe as 'a dizzy blonde'. For the last two months, Crash had been going round Cairo with Amanda. But Lucie knew from old Lorrimer that Amanda Portlake could never be any good to Crash. She was just one of those thin, feverish, cocktail-drinking young women, who danced through life to the tune of a fox-trot, and lived for the next party.

Lucie felt deadly tired. She was also nearing the stage when she wanted to stop trying to be philosophical or brave, to break down and have 'a good cry'. If only someone would come!

Ah, those blue, poignant skies . . . so soon to change to fiery red . . . then, after the exquisite dream of the sunset, sudden darkness, the chill of the starry night, alone in a car in the desert. It wasn't a very pleasant prospect. And suddenly Lucie felt that she could not stay here a moment longer. She must leave the car and walk, walk until she found some kind of road, some kind of clue, which would put her on to the route for Cairo.

With the last cherished cigarette between her lips, Lucie began to stride forward, leaving the poor Morris behind her. She must get back. She must find people, civilisation, again. It was all there waiting for her. She could not sit down like a little fool and starve.

For half an hour she walked, straining her eyes for the first sign of a building in the distance . . . Surely at any moment she would see the tall spires of the Citadel rising up into the sky, or the Pyramids. Yes, surely in a moment or two she would see those gigantic Pyramids, which had once been the resting-place of the great Pharaohs, thousands of years ago.

She began to stumble, to falter, every limb aching, face drenched with perspiration, brown curls sticking damply to her forehead. There was a pain in her side. She was done, she told herself, and could not go on. And suddenly she dropped down in a little heap on the warm sand, hid her face on her arms and began to cry.

When she lifted her head again, she realised that she must have drifted from tears into sleep, the sleep of total exhaustion. And now the thing that she had feared had happened. The sun had gone down, and there was a violet darkness brooding over the desert. A darkness that made her loneliness feel even more intense. Yet beauty was here in the crystal light of the big cold stars; and the faint crescent of moon, which hung like a sickle in the indigo sky.

Lucie staggered on to her feet. She was cold, shivering from head to foot, and her limbs were cramped. Desperately she looked around her, her heart pounding with all the old fears. She might never be found. And this might mean—the end! Lucie raised her despairing young face to the stars.

'I don't want to die,' she whispered. 'I don't want to be left here to die in the wilderness. I love life. And I want to know all the joy of living and loving . . . love that I have pictured only in my dreams!'

No answer. Nothing for Lucie but that infinite stillness about her, and the melancholy baying of dogs.

Then, suddenly, that blank silence lifted. She heard the sound of an engine . . . the powerful humming noise of a powerful motor . . . and in the distance a flash of a light . . . the headlights from a car coming in her direction.

Hope surged wildly in Lucie's heart. She began to stumble over the desert in the direction of that light, praying madly that whoever was in the car, Arab or Englishman, would see her, take pity on her, convey her back to the safety of Cairo.

And it seemed in no time that the powerful

beams of the headlamps of that car flung a white ribbon of light across her, blinding her sight. She sobbed wildly:

'Oh, stop, please stop!'

Then she heard a man's voice. She did not know what he said. She was semi-conscious then. She only knew that a man had jumped out of the car and had put a steadying arm around her shoulder. He was saying:

'Good God! How on earth did you get here! It's Lucie Bryant, *Lucie* . . . How on earth did you get here, my dear?'

Then Lucie knew who it was. That voice belonged to Crash . . . Crash Lorrimer. This was Crash's famous Lagonda racing-car which he had been driving at his usual demon's pace. It was Crash who lifted her into the seat beside the wheel and put a cushion behind her head.

'You poor kid,' he said. 'You're in the devil of a state. However long have you been out here, and what are you doing all by yourself?'

She could not speak for a few moments. Her relief was too enormous. And not only was it a wild relief to know that she was safe . . . but a thrill to be sitting in his car . . . to know that it was *he* who had found her. He had uncorked a flask of brandy and was making her take a sip from it.

'I always carry this in case of accidents,' he explained. 'Come along . . . don't choke . . . it will soon put you right.'

She drank some brandy and felt hysteria

gradually subsiding. She grew calm, able to smile, to talk to him. She said:

'I never thought it would be you who would find me.'

He stood beside her, leaning over the door of the car, smoking a cigarette, regarding her half with amusement, half with concern. He had so often seen little Lucie in his father's office. He had never taken much notice of her; thought her a bit quiet and dull. And yet tonight, in the starlight, there was quite a lot of beauty to be found in her face, he thought. A heart-shaped little face with wide, brave eyes, and a sensitive mouth. He knew that his father was a great admirer of Lucie. She was his right hand in the office, capable beyond her twenty-one years. But Crash had never admired capability or efficiency in a woman. In his opinion girls were just meant to be lovely— and spoiled. Like Amanda!

'How did you get here?' he asked her.

She explained how she had brought the old Morris for a picnic and lost her way.

'But you mad child!' he chided. 'You know you should never drive off the road without desert-tyres.'

Lucie pushed the brown, tangled curls back from her forehead. Her face, which a few moments ago had been white and pinched with exhaustion, was warm now, flushed, vital. Crash was standing there, looking down at her with those attractive blue eyes of his in a way

9

that would make any woman's heart turn over. And now that all her fears were ended, she felt only the glamour of the moment . . . of the wonderful night in the desert under the great Egyptian stars. And Crash, Crash who had come to her rescue.

'I know now how idiotic I was,' she said, 'and what incredible luck I have had being picked up by you. What are *you* doing out here, anyhow?'

He gave her a school-boy grin, which made him look younger than his twenty-five years, and did not answer for a moment. He was too busy lighting a cigarette for her and another for himself. She regarded him a bit dazedly. He wore grey flannels and a blue pullover, with a silk scarf around his brown throat. Was there ever a more attractive face, she wondered. He had a pure Greek profile and a mouth that could be tender and gay and perhaps a little cruel; as beautifully shaped as a woman's.

His own father called him spoiled, despaired of him. He had a crazy streak. Yet Lucie was positive that he was not vicious. There was strength in the squareness of that cleft chin, and in the frank directness of his eyes. He wanted a firm hand and he didn't get it, that was all. He had his own way too much, even in the Army. Too much money and spare time . . . a gay aimless sort of existence that a soldier can lead in a military station in Cairo.

10

He was being particularly kind to her now. He made her drink a little more brandy, found a rug at the back of the Lagonda, wrapped it around her, and told her how he had come across her.

There had been no polo at the Club this afternoon. Last night the Royal Buckinghamshires had given what he called 'a monster party', and this morning he had suffered from a 'hang-over'. And most of this afternoon he had slept. He had wakened with a bad head and felt so rotten that he had decided to take the car and drive out here 'hell for leather', as he called it.

'I thought it would freshen me up, and it has. And with desert-tyres I can just go anywhere, right off the road. That's why I ran into you, Lucie. But you must never do a thing like this again.'

She smiled and shook her head.

'I never will!'

He came round to the other side of the car and took his place at the wheel.

'Feeling all right now?'

'More or less.'

Then he noticed that she was rubbing her foot. He peered down and saw a glimpse of white ankle through a torn silk stocking, and a smear of red. He clicked his tongue.

'You've hurt yourself. Let me look.'

'It's nothing,' she said. 'Just a scratch. I stumbled and grazed my ankle against a stone.'

11

He insisted upon examining the injury.

'You know what Egypt's like. You've got to be careful of scratches. They soon go bad on you. Lift your foot up a minute.'

The next moment, Lucie found herself without shoe or stocking, and Crash was wrapping a silk handkerchief around the wound. Those fingers of his were hard, yet sensitive. It was mingled thrill and pain to feel the contact of them. And he was thinking:

'She's a plucky kid. It's quite a nasty gash, but she doesn't fuss.'

He said:

'Shall we go and inspect your car, or shall I take you straight back, and get Fagan from the garage in Abbassia to tow in the wreck tomorrow?'

'Yes, if it doesn't cost too much,' she nodded. 'Otherwise it will have to be left here for the pie-dogs! I can hardly afford it as it is.'

Crash Lorrimer was silent for a moment. Somehow it seemed all wrong that a young and pretty girl shouldn't be able to afford what she wanted. He, who was used to spending money like water; used to seeing women like Amanda Portlake spend it for him, rarely stopped to think of the financial hardships that beset those who worked as Lucie did for her living. He registered a mental vow to ask his father to stick a bit on her salary this month, so that she could have the little car repaired.

With a careless gesture he put a hand over

12

hers, then picked it up and pressed it with an exclamation:

'Good lord, you're still frozen!'

'I'll be all right,' she said.

But her head was drooping a little and she could no longer see the stars. Those hours of stumbling about in the desert, believing herself to be lost, had had a mental as well as a physical effect upon her.

Crash Lorrimer could never bear to see a woman suffer. All that was best in him came to the surface. He wrapped the rug still closer around the shivering young body, started up the car and drove Lucie swiftly over the sands and on to the beaten track which he knew so well.

'The sooner you get home to bed, the better, my child,' he said.

She was only semi-conscious by the time they reached the town and Heliopolis, the suburb in which she lived. But in a dim way she was conscious of that warm magnetic presence at her side; of Crash's solicitude. She thought:

'People say he is inconsequent . . . selfish . . . but I think he must be the kindest person in the world . . .'

He would not let her walk. He insisted upon lifting her right up in his arms and carried her to her room in the pension. He laid her on her bed and covered her with his rug.

'Keep it,' he said. 'I'll collect it sometime in

the morning. And you're not to go down to the office. I'll ring up Dad and tell him what happened to you.'

She struggled to thank him, to protest that she would be quite well enough to work tomorrow. But Crash was masterful.

'You've got to have the day off. I'll see the old man gives it to you.'

While he stood there, he looked round and felt suddenly ashamed of himself because he knew so little about the poverties and difficulties of others. Here was a very decent, pretty kid, obviously of good birth and breeding, facing life alone in Cairo . . . and with just this room for her home. Unattractive, pathetic because of Lucie's obvious attempts to make the best of it. A bowl of roses . . . some photographs . . . a few books . . . some Egyptian embroidery against the white walls. But nothing luxurious. Nothing that began to resemble the extravagantly appointed house in Gezira, in which Amanda Portlake lived. Amanda who was never without masses of flowers, bottles of scent, and huge boxes of chocolates.

Crash Lorrimer had no interest in his father's secretary. But that night when he left her, he went down into the town and ordered an enormous bunch of carnations to be sent to her address. He had it sent anonymously. He did not wish to embarrass Lucie by putting his name to the bouquet.

14

But Lucie knew whence those flowers had come. Ill and exhausted though she was that night, with a slight touch of fever, she was inordinately happy. Crash's rug covered her, Crash's silk handkerchief, which he had wrapped round her ankle, lay on the table beside her, and Crash's flowers decorated the room. It seemed like a miracle. And she realised, too, that the shadowy adoration which she had felt for him before, had tonight developed into an overwhelming and passionate love.

She always slept with the curtains pulled back from the window which was wide open. Tonight for a long time she lay awake. She could see her cherished flowers which *he* had sent, flooded by the pure and brilliant beauty of the moonlight. She could see those great stars which had shone over her and Crash in the desert earlier in the evening. She could hear the distant plaintive droning of a native voice . . . an Egyptian boatman singing from a felucca as it drifted down the Nile.

'All-ah! All-ah!'

An unceasing cry to God. It found an echo in her heart tonight when at length she drifted into sleep. And she had the curious psychic feeling that Crash Lorrimer, gay, irresponsible, reckless Crash was echoing that cry. And for the most shadowy and inexplicable reasons, she was afraid for him.

II

Lucie did not have her day's holiday. Nothing would induce her to take one unless she were really too ill to move. Next morning found her at her typewriter. But it found her not quite so engrossed in her work as usual. She kept thinking about yesterday . . . those glittering desert stars . . . and Crash's arm protectingly around her.

From her desk she could see below the busy street . . . the motley gathering of people. European and native; Egyptians who wore the scarlet tasselled tarboosh on their heads; Arabs in their long voluminous robes and turbans; camels laden with sugar-cane padding incongruously in between sleek expensive cars. And over all, the warm drenching sunshine, the vivid blue of the sky that *could* only be Egypt.

A bell summoned her into the next room. She took her pad and pencil and presented herself to her employer.

'Well, here you are,' said Edgar Lorrimer kindly, smiling at his young secretary. 'Crash told me I darned nearly lost you in the desert yesterday.'

Her face flooded with colour.

'I think I might still be there if he hadn't found me.'

'Sure you're none the worse?'

'Quite, Mr Lorrimer.'

'Well, well, then we'll get on with the job,' he said. 'We've got to tackle the insurance company for the boy. Young fool, last week-end he had a crash on the Alexandria road. One of these days he'll be killed. He didn't do himself or the car in this time, but he buckled in the other fellow's mud-guards. When will he learn common sense?'

Lucie's gaze travelled to a leather-framed photograph on her employer's desk. Crash in full-dress uniform with his hand on the hilt of his sword. The most handsome and spectacular figure. She could not bear to think that he wasted his time and his life. And she was sorry for the old man, too. He had had a tragic life. Success in his job and tons of money, but absolute failure in his personal life. An adored wife who had died young and Conrad his son and heir . . . 'Crash'. . . the only one left to him, a continual source of tribulation.

'Lucie,' said old Lorrimer, 'when do you think my boy will calm down and put an end to all this tom-foolery?'

'I wish I knew.'

Old Lorrimer grunted.

'What he wants is a wife.'

Lucie coloured faintly.

'*He* doesn't think so, does he?'

'No, but it's time he did. None of your

Amanda Portlakes, but a sensible, healthy-minded girl with good influence. A fine woman like his mother. A girl like . . . like . . .'

He stopped and grunted again. It had been on the tip of his tongue to say:

'*A girl like you . . . !*'

He switched off the subject of his son and began to dictate his business-letters. Lucie sat at his side, her pencil slipping over the pad swiftly and easily. And old Lorrimer thought today as he had thought many times in the past, that it was a pity the boy didn't turn his attentions to a girl like *this*.

Perhaps if Crash saw more of little Lucie, he would become interested. He ought to throw them together. *That* was the thing.

In the middle of a business-letter, old Lorrimer's thoughts strayed to Crash. Suddenly he said:

'Has the boy ever taken you out?'

Lucie's face flushed scarlet.

'Gracious me, no.'

'Time he did.'

Lucie laughed.

'Of *course* not.'

'Why "of course not"? There's the Benevolent Ball at the Embassy next week. I'd like him to take you to it.'

Lucie's heart almost stopped beating. The idea of going to a ball with Crash was just too delirious . . . one of those dreams which could never come true. Old Lorrimer's suggestion

18

staggered her. It was *absurd!*

'Crash has his own girl-friends. *Please* don't mention me to him, in connection with the ball . . .' A bit anxiously the old man looked at her.

'Don't you like him?'

She did not answer. How could she? How could she tell Edgar Lorrimer that she was desperately in love with his son? But Edgar Lorrimer was a student of human-nature as well as a businessman. Her silence and the sudden glow in those golden hazel eyes of hers was enough for him. That young devil, Crash, all women fell for him! The old man made a mental note that he would fix up that ball for Lucie.

Lucie was still in the office at four, that same afternoon. The rest of the staff were there, too, but old Lorrimer had gone. He had had a business lunch at the Continental-Savoy, and not returned from it.

Lucie finished copying out her shorthand notes, and suddenly she was aware of fatigue. She felt slack, unlike herself. She put the cover on her machine and finding a compactum in her bag, powdered her nose and tidied a few truant curls. Her face still bore a tan from last summer's sun, but she was not looking well. She was not *feeling* very well. And she knew that the cause was not so much physical as mental. She was depressed. Her spirits were at low-ebb. She found herself wondering how

19

long life would continue in its present monotony.

Two years ago, at nineteen, with her father alive, and herself only just out in Egypt from an English school, she had been having a grand time. The sort of good time a girl can have in Cairo. Plenty of young officers to take her about. Bathing, tennis, picnics on the Nile, and in the desert. Lots of healthy harmless fun. But all that fun had finished for Lucie. Life held nothing but work now . . . work from nine till five. After that, 'some fun' if she wanted it, certainly. She knew people in Cairo. There were plenty of young men in the Army who still wanted to take her out. But for most times she was too tired after a heavy day at the office to do more than spend a quiet evening with a book at the pension where she lived. If she went out, she found late nights made her dull and heavy for the next day's job.

The office door burst open, and Lucie jumped to her feet, startled, shy as a fawn whose retreat has been broken in upon. The object of her thoughts came into that office and hailed her in a gay cheerful voice.

'Hullo! So I've caught you, have I? I wondered if you'd gone.'

'Caught me?' repeated Lucie. 'What do you want me for?'

'To see if you contemplate any more picnics in the desert.'

Crash Lorrimer grinned at her. Grinned like

a schoolboy and looked rather like one, Lucie told herself, in his grey flannels, dark blue blazer and striped silk muffler around his brown throat. The handsome, impudent face bore little traces of the debaucheries attributed to him. Except for a tiny network of lines round those handsome eyes, Crash looked as healthy and tireless as a trained athlete.

'I've been playing squash at the Club,' he said. 'Then I nipped into a taxi and cracked along here. I suppose you've heard I bashed in the front wings of some Frenchman's car the other day?'

Lucie had recovered her equilibrium now. She tried to smoke her cigarette with unapparent concern as she talked to him.

'Yes, I know.'

'Dad's been on to the Insurance Company, I hear.'

'Yes, this morning. But you must go along to sign a form.'

'Yes, I saw the old man after lunch down at the Club. But I wanted my game of squash. I'll call in at the Insurance Office on my way back to the garrison.'

'I do wish you would be careful in your car,' said Lucie.

'You've no *idea* how careful I am,' he said.

'So it seems,' said Lucie.

'Now, now,' he laughed, 'no sarcasm!'

'Well, one day you won't get away with it.'

'You're just the mouthpiece of my paternal

parent. But don't worry, Lucie. I've got a charmed life.'

'You shouldn't challenge fate,' she said, hastily.

'Would you mourn for me, little Lucie? Would you drop a bundle of shorthand-notes on my grave?'

She coloured and laughed.

'You are absurd.'

'So are you. Absolutely too strong-minded and decorous for one so young and beautiful. The perfect secretary! Dad thinks you're the cat's whiskers, you know.'

She was tongue-tied under his praise. He added:

'None the worse for last night's sensational episode, eh?'

'None.'

'Had the Morris towed in?'

'Yes.'

'Why didn't you take the day off today as I wanted you to do?'

'Because I've got to get on with my job.'

He looked at her with some amusement. She was so very serious, and so self-conscious with him. Yet he began to think that, well-dressed, she would be pretty good to look at. She had marvellous ankles and those hazel eyes of hers were quite lovely. She just wanted 'bringing out'. He had a sudden lazy effect to bring her out, himself. So he started to flirt outrageously.

'We must have another desert adventure, only next time we'll get lost together.'

She tried to laugh and to appear unconcerned.

'How ridiculous you are.'

'Not nearly as ridiculous as you, to spend your half-days alone. Dad was saying at lunch-time, it's time you came out of your shell and I agree. How about dining with me one night, or would that bore you?'

Lucie caught her breath. She hadn't bargained for this. The violent colour stained her face but she tried to answer him coolly.

'Oh, I . . . I hardly ever go out at nights. One can't burn the candles at both ends.'

'My dear little Miss Victorian,' he teased her, 'you're just too sweet, but that won't wash with me. I burn the candles both ends continually, and I assure you it's *quite* simple.'

'Is it?' she said, helplessly.

'Besides,' he continued, 'you're much too attractive to spend the whole of your life sitting over a typewriter, or taking down dull, dry notes for Dad.'

'It's my job . . .'

'A pretty girl has another job . . . almost a sacred duty . . . to improve the shining hour for lonely young officers in foreign stations.'

That made her laugh. She shook her head.

'You're not trying to pretend you're a lonely young man?'

He folded his arms across his chest.

'Of course I am! Lonely amidst the gay and fashionable throng that surrounds me. I say, that sounds good, I ought to have been a writer.'

'You're absurd.'

'You've said that before. But listen to me, Lucie, and take note! Get out that pad and pencil, write the following words: "On Thursday the 19th February, you are invited to the Benevolent Ball at the Embassy as the guest of Mr Conrad Lorrimer of the Royal Buckinghamshires. Whereto, on the aforesaid date, you will dine with Mr Lorrimer at Shepheard's Grill, prior to the ball."'

Lucie remained silent a moment. She knew perfectly well in that moment that her employer had carried out his threat of this morning. He had said that he would ask his son to take her to the Ball. She was furious about it. Yet a thrill of purest excitement ran through her veins. How *gorgeous!* . . . What a wonderful evening for her! To go alone with Crash, to the Embassy Ball. She could not help wondering why he had agreed to take her? What about Amanda?

At the very moment, Crash was thinking about his Amanda, annoyed because she wouldn't be in Cairo on February 19th. She had to fly to Alexandria with her father that very day to meet relatives, passing through Alex from India. Crash had been at a loose end when his father had made the suggestion that he should take his secretary to that Ball. Half-heartedly he had promised to do so, just to please the old man. To appease him, too, for crashing up the car again. He knew what a lot the old boy thought of Lucie. But now Crash made the invitation quite earnestly. It would be something new in his life, an evening out with a funny shy little thing like Lucie. He wondered what sort of dress she would wear. He could picture her looking rather a pet if she took pains with herself. And he was rather gratified to note that her reactions to himself were distinctly 'forthcoming'. She liked him. That was obvious. She was thrilled.

She began to protest that she couldn't possibly go with him to the Ball. He drowned the feeble protests and became the dominant and victorious male.

'Of course you'll come. Refuse me and I shall have you flung out of the Near-East Petroleum Company into the dark shades of the Egyptian gutter.'

Her slim body shook with helpless laughter.

'You *are* impossible.'

He slid off the edge of the desk and stood smiling down at her with his handsome blue eyes.

'It's a date. Shepheard's Grill, nine o'clock next Thursday night.'

'Thanks awfully,' was all she could say; and hoped he did not guess how wildly her heart was thumping.

'I must go,' he said. 'Can I give you a lift? I'll drop you at your pension.'

'Thank you, but I usually take the Brown Tram.'

He was shocked and said so. Trams in Cairo were not fit for girls like Lucie, he said. He was going to take a taxi to Helmieh, which was the headquarters of the Royal Buckinghamshires. He would drop her in Heliopolis, the suburb where she lived, en route, he said.

'How's the little foot, Lucie?'

'It was nothing,' she said. 'I put some plaster on it. By the way, I've got your handkerchief. I'll wash it and give it back to you.'

His blue handsome eyes smiled down at her.

'If you wash it yourself, I'll never use it again. I'll frame it!'

She gave a little chuckling laugh. He liked that laugh—it was so unaffected. In fact, he was in the mood to like Lucie.

'Come on,' he said, 'the car's waiting.'

It was altogether an exciting end to Lucie's day. She accompanied Crash to the Insurance Office, and then there was the long drive through Cairo to Heliopolis. He was charming to her. Oh, vital, amusing, gorgeous young man! How could anyone be cross with him for long? It would be so easy to forgive him— *anything!*

Once back at her pension, Lucie gave way to the excitement which she had tried to conceal from Crash. Out came her account book . . . a wild rush to see how much money she had left over from last week's salary; and what she had in her savings bank. Could she afford a new dress? A 'set' at the best hairdressers? A manicure?

Whether she could afford it or not, she must do it all. There followed a delirious hour for Lucie. The practical, the economic young woman who was Edgar Lorrimer's secretary, had become infected with some of Crash's irresponsibility. A large lump of her small savings went into the new dress. (How could she possibly be seen with Crash at the Embassy in an old one?) She had a consultation with the little French dressmaker who made most of her clothes. She wanted a Victorian dress with tight bodice falling off the shoulders and a full skirt. She would go down to the Mousky tomorrow, that native bazaar where one could pick up cheap and lovely materials. She would buy some brocade, and Mademoiselle would fashion a creation from it, with her clever fingers. A rosy-pinky colour would suit her, thought Lucie, and she would wear pink roses in her hair. And she would get out the cultured pearls which had been poor Daddy's last present to her while he was still well-off, and her mother's diamond bracelet. The only treasures she possessed. They must all come out for Crash's benefit. She must look *marvellous* for the most sought-after young man in Cairo.

Old Lorrimer found a new quality in his secretary that following morning. A quality of excitement which animated her small face and quickened her movements. She had become suddenly a live wire. He knew why. And he was glad of it. Why, the child was head-over-ears in love with his boy. Damn it! Crash would be a lunatic if he didn't see what she was worth, and make the most of his opportunities.

He slipped a five pound note into Lucie's hand that evening.

'Just a little bonus, my dear. You've done a lot of hard work for me lately. Go and get something pretty for yourself for the ball.'

She thanked him, starry-eyed, grateful. That five pounds would solve all her financial difficulties and the old man thought:

'It's a damn shame to think what it means to her. Whilst that yellow-haired imbecile my son runs round with wouldn't think it a gift unless it was ten times five.'

From that moment onward, until the night of the ball, Lucie lived like one in a dream. She did not see Crash again. She only heard his voice on the telephone one afternoon when he wanted to speak to his father. He reminded her that she was meeting him and talked a lot of nonsense about 'longing for the day'. Flirting with her, disgracefully. She knew it wasn't more than that. But she loved him. God, how she loved him! And how she wished that she *didn't*.

III

From the very start of their evening together, it was a success. To begin with, she was conscious that she had achieved a little triumph with her appearance. Mademoiselle had not failed her and Crash Lorrimer was agreeably surprised when he saw his partner for the evening walking across the lounge of the hotel toward him. A small graceful figure, with rich folds of pink and silver brocades (Mousky, of course) flaring out from a tiny waist down to the tip of small silvershod feet.

A tight little bodice showed the charming curve of her breasts. The sloping shoulders were bare, and her face was like a flower on the long lily slope of her throat. Why she was really entrancing! A transformation from the quiet little mouse he had always seen in Dad's office. He liked a woman's hair to be sleek and subtle, and little Lucie was fresh from the hands of the best coiffeur . . . chestnut brown curls on the top of her head, pink roses pinned to them, as she had planned.

'You look a dream,' Crash told her enthusiastically. 'I'm proud of you, little Miss Victorian. A *real* Victorian tonight, only, thank God, you haven't brought your chaperone.'

'Shall I need one?' she laughed at him.

'Well, you know the sort of reputation I've got.'

He laughed down at her and she felt her knees go all wobbly. He had no *right* to look at her like that when he was supposed to be in love with Amanda Portlake. It was a warm intimate look such as a woman expects from her lover. Lucie thought:

'He's not *my* lover, and never will be!'

But she wasn't going to be depressed about it. She was much too happy tonight. Much too proud. She saw all the other women in the hotel passing side-long glances at her escort as they passed them. He was divine in full dress-uniform, his dark hair smooth and glistening tonight. As romantic a figure as any girl could dream of in those cherry-coloured, tight-fitting overalls and short little jacket with its gleaming buttons; the gold chain epaulettes and stiff white collar and tie. Devastating to Lucie's adoring heart.

He set himself out to be charming to her. There was no more perfect host. He had ordered a special dinner and there were special flowers on the table. Everybody knew him. The entire staff bowed and scraped before Mr Lorrimer, who threw his money about so gracefully and recklessly, and for whom there must be the best champagne, the finest cigars.

At the Embassy, Lucie felt that she was living in a fairy-tale. Starry-eyed and happy, she danced with her adored Crash (of course he was a perfect dancer), and watched all the other officers in their gay, sleek uniforms with their well-dressed soignée partners and the Ambassador and his wife, themselves. Lucie had never before been to such a brilliant function. She was entranced. But she told herself that she would have been just as entranced in the arms of Crash Lorrimer in the most humble surroundings.

She made the most of her evening, conscious that Crash was as fully determined to enjoy himself as she was. He showered her with compliments, with praises for her dancing, her appearance, trying to turn her head a little, just to amuse himself. He drank plenty of champagne. Flushed, handsome, sparkling as they danced to lilting music played by a regimental band. In between dances, they sat out and he bought her drinks and ices; smoked with her, talked confidentially to her, treated her as though she was the only woman in Cairo who counted.

Lucie lived life to the full, rising to dizzy heights that never-to-be-forgotten evening. She need envy no woman.

'Hullo, Crash . . .'

'Darling, how are you . . .?'

Dozens of pretty girls spoke to him as they passed; looked at him with knowing, intimate little looks as though they had all been in Lucie's shoes at some time or other. But she didn't care. He was *hers* for this evening and she gloried in it.

If Crash Lorrimer was bored with Lucie, he did not show it. He was not so very bored. She amused him because she was unspoiled and *very* responsive to a look or a word. She was quite an engaging little thing, he decided, and definitely pretty in her brocade dress, with that Victorian coiffeur. But, of course, he wished he had his Amanda here. Amanda made a fellow howl with laughter. She drank too much, but she was damned amusing. If it had been Amanda, he would have taken her along to a cabaret after the Ball. But he thought perhaps he had better take little Lucie home.

So at two o'clock in the morning, they drove in a taxi from the Embassy back to Heliopolis, Crash yawning a bit, Lucie still in a state of enchantment, tired and blissfully happy.

His arm slipped around her. It seemed natural to draw the slim little figure close to him. Equally natural to drop a kiss on those pretty brown curls. And then, perhaps, the nearness of her and the sweet scent of her roses, and the fact that she trembled under his touch, made Crash do what any other man would have done in his place. He kissed her on the lips. Taking fire from that caress, enjoying the sweetness of her lips, he held her a little more closely and roughly and kissed her with real passion, not once but several times.

She was all his in those dizzying seconds. With arms about his neck, she returned the kisses as passionately as they were given. She

32

had never known before that it could be such ecstasy in a man's embrace. Crash's hands were hard and possessive and he said crazy little things to her, against her mouth:

'Oh, you darling . . . how sweet you are! . . . little flower-face . . . Lucie, little lovely one . . .'

But she was inarticulate. Blindly adoring him, putting her whole soul into that embrace.

The next moment they were outside her pension in the quiet Heliopolis street. Then Crash recovered himself and drew away. The roses had fallen from her hair on to the floor. As Crash stepped out, his foot trod upon them, crushing them out of recognition.

Under the stars and cool night air, he bade Lucie goodnight more formally. Passion had died in him. He was a little remorseful about those kisses, so he touched her hand with his lips and said:

'All my thanks, for a grand evening. See you again, one day soon.'

That was all. She stammered goodnight, and watched the taxi carry away the handsome young man in his gorgeous uniform. With him he carried away her heart. All the ecstasy of the evening was gone for her now. She stood there for a moment rather like a flower that had wilted in the heat of the evening. Pale, big-eyed and unsmiling.

She knew perfectly well that she had been a fool to surrender even a fraction of her soul with those kisses. She knew they had meant nothing to Crash Lorrimer.

'You're a fool, Lucie,' she fiercely admonished herself. 'And you've no pride or you wouldn't waste your emotions on a man whom you *know* hasn't the slightest use for you.'

In her bedroom, she took off the brocade dress and the silver slippers and then looked for the flowers in her hair. She found they had gone.

For an instant, eyes shut, hands clenched, she remembered the hard pressure of his lips, the wild thrill of his embrace.

Then she flung herself face downwards on her bed and burst into tears.

IV

That next morning when his secretary presented herself to take the morning's letters, Edgar Lorrimer asked:

'Did you enjoy the ball, my dear?'

She answered lightly:

'Oh, yes, thank you, Mr Lorrimer. It was grand fun!'

But he, looking at her shrewdly through horn-rimmed glasses, thought that she looked different, somehow, almost matured in some curious way. Her pallor, those violet shadows under her eyes, were they merely traces of a late night, or had the child been crying? He wasn't sure!

And during that week that followed, he wasn't at all sure what had happened between Lucie and his son on that night at the Embassy. When he questioned her, she was evasive. She just continued to say it 'had been grand fun'. But the tell-tale colour would flood her cheeks, and morning after morning, she arrived at the office looking pale and tired and rather miserable.

Of course, old Lorrimer knew what it was . . . she was in love with young Crash. But there seemed no further talk about him taking her out again. The young fool hadn't made use of his opportunities after all. Whenever his father saw him, Crash was in the company of that hard, blonde young female whom old Lorrimer had detested at first sight.

Came an afternoon when he suggested that his secretary should have an extra afternoon off, go down to Gezira Club with him—that charming Club where the Army gathered daily—and watch a polo-match in which Crash was playing.

'You've been overworking and you look tired out,' he said briskly when Lucie hesitated to accept. 'Come along. Put the cover on your typewriter, my dear, and get your coat. The car's waiting outside.'

She went with him, not only glad to have the holiday because it was a gorgeous, sunny day, but thrilled at the idea of seeing Crash on the polo-ground, and in the company of his father. It was an honour that old Lorrimer had never paid her before. All that week she had starved for a sight of Crash. The only time she had seen him, he had passed her by, driving a new racing-car which he had bought, extravagantly, because he could not wait for the Lagonda to be on the road again. And of course there was a fair-haired girl at his side—the inevitable, smartly-dressed, much made-up Amanda!

In secret bitterness, Lucie had once again admonished herself for being a fool. Amanda was Crash's 'girl-friend'. That ball at the Embassy when he had kissed her, Lucie, so passionately, had been to him only an amusing interlude.

She sat beside old Lorrimer watching the polo with much interest—a wild thrill in her heart because she could follow the familiar, graceful figure of Crash on his polo-pony. A white-clad supple body which seemed one with the grey Arab which he was riding. Hooves thundering past her, stick raised and then, crack . . . the little ball went spinning across the polo-ground toward the goal. Crash riding like mad, wheeling and circling, the finest player in the team.

Old Lorrimer also followed the game, but he was not concentrating on the figure of his son. He was busy watching the rapt expression on his little secretary's face. He could read what lay in her eyes. He thought:

'*I* felt like that about the boy's mother when I first met her thirty years ago. I wish to *God* Crash had eyes in his head, and I could see this girl married to him before I die!'

When the match ended—Crash had led the Royal Buckinghamshires to victory—he came up to his father, wiping his flushed handsome face and dark head, vigorously. He looked surprised when he saw the girl beside the old man. Little Lucie, eh? What was *she* doing here with the old man? Not looking quite as ravishing as in her Victorian dress at the ball. Her Jaeger coat was a bit shabby. But he liked the dark blue tucked-in scarf, and her little blue sandals. She was really quite a pretty kid in her way.

'How are you, dad? And how's our Lucie?' he greeted them, gaily.

'Well played, my boy,' said old Lorrimer. 'Now look here, I've got to go off to a meeting. How about giving Lucie a cup of tea?'

'Oh, no, please . . .' began Lucie, flushing, awkward, and wishing that her heart would not beat so wildly because Crash's blue eyes were upon her. (Was he remembering those kisses as *she* remembered them?)

But Crash was remembering little beyond the fact that he had a date with Amanda at the Semiramis Hotel where there was a *thé dansant* today.

'I say, I'm awfully sorry,' he said,

apologetically, 'but I've unfortunately promised to meet Amanda, otherwise ...'

'It doesn't matter at all,' cut in Lucie, quickly, and added in an agony of embarrassment: 'I couldn't stay to tea anyhow. I've got an appointment with a girl at Groppi's.' (She mentioned the name of a popular tea-shop in the town.)

Crash looked relieved. He didn't want to be rude to the little girl. He waved goodbye and went off to the changing-rooms. Pale, but with her curly head high, Lucie walked with her employer to his car.

'I'll drive you to Groppi's,' the old man said. But his lips were grim and to himself he was saying:

'She hasn't a date there at all. She's just made it up. The boy's a *fool.* Amanda Portlake! That mercenary little ...'

He muttered a word to himself that he would not have liked Lucie to hear.

He felt irritated beyond measure. That son of his who had ridden so recklessly and so well on the polo-ground this afternoon ... was he not, figuratively speaking, riding to his ruin? Helped on by women like Amanda ... drinking too hard ... *living* too hard? And later when he came into his inheritance, there would be no end to his follies. With all that money and no decent woman at his side to guide him, the boy might be ruined altogether.

Was it the heat or just a trick of his heart,

38

Lorrimer wondered, that made him falter and clutch his breast as he entered his car? Lucie saw him go ashen-grey and the sweat start out on his brow. She uttered an exclamation of dismay:

'Are you ill? Oh, Mr Lorrimer, what's the matter?'

He sank panting on to the seat beside her. For a moment he held on to her cool, kind little hand. It gave him comfort. His eyes closed and he had a queer vision, in that moment, of the boy's mother . . . Kathleen, his lost darling . . . She had been small and sweet and a little like this girl at his side.

'I'm all right,' he said, gruffly, 'tell the man to drive on into the town.'

But after he left Lucie at her tea-shop, he did not go straight to the office. He went to his doctor . . . an Englishman who had been attending him ever since he had lived in Egypt.

And within an hour, Edgar Lorrimer knew that it was not his fancy . . . not just the hot sun, nor fatigue that had shot that agonising pain through his heart.

He was going the way his father had gone before him, with *angina*. He had asked the doctor for the truth and he had been told. Work and worry and too many years in the heat of the Sudan had 'got him'. He hadn't very much longer to live. This afternoon had only been a warning. The next time it might be a real attack and then . . . goodbye.

For himself he was not afraid. He was a tired-out old man and he believed that on the Other Side, his Kathleen would be waiting for him. But there was Crash. That lovable, reckless idiot of a boy. How could he rest in peace, knowing that Crash meant to pursue his reckless way . . . in the company of girls like Amanda!

He thought of Lucie; of her courage in spite of hard work and loneliness; Lucie with her proud little head held high in the face of defeat . . . defeat such as she had met this afternoon, in the face of her hopeless love. And suddenly his mind was made up. And once made up, not to be revoked.

Edgar Lorrimer paid another unusual visit that same afternoon. A visit to Martin Spenser, his solicitor in Cairo.

'I am a sick man . . . in fact a dying one,' he said, 'and I want to make an entirely new Will.'

Martin Spenser looked surprised. He had made Lorrimer's Will for him twenty years ago, since when it had not been altered. And he had left everything, unreservedly, to his only son.

'Not going to cut the lad out, are you?' he asked with a smile.

'No,' said Edgar Lorrimer, 'that is . . . not if he does what I want him to do.'

'What's that, my friend?'

'Takes the wife I've chosen for him,' said Lorrimer abruptly.

So, on that February evening, when the sun set in a red blaze of glory over the calm waters of the Nile, one of the wealthiest men in Egypt made a Will leaving his entire fortune to his son, Conrad Edgar Lorrimer, on condition that he married within twelve months of probate being granted the girl who was at the moment his private secretary, Lucie Bryant of Heliopolis, Cairo. Failing that, the said Conrad Edgar Lorrimer must forfeit his inheritance except for an annual sum of two hundred and fifty a year.

'Which, of course,' old Spenser remarked, 'would barely be enough to support his polo ponies.'

'I agree,' said Edgar Lorrimer, 'and it would also mean that he would have to resign his commission. But I don't think it will come to that. I fancy he'll prefer to marry my secretary and live as a rich man.'

'You're taking a risk,' said his lawyer. 'You're forcing his hand and he won't like it, and neither will she.'

'She's in love with him,' was Lorrimer's reply, 'and she'll look after him till the end of his days. She'll *make* him, that child, if I know anything about her.'

'H'm,' said Martin Spenser, and added to himself: 'And if I know anything about young Crash Lorrimer, he may marry the girl, but long before *she* can make him, *he'll* break her!'

But Edgar Lorrimer saw only the

redemption of his son and the ultimate happiness of Lucie when, twenty-four hours later, he put his signature to that new, fateful Will.

V

The next heart-attack that seized Edgar Lorrimer in a month's time, did not kill him. But it put a permanent end to his activities in the office and sent him to his bed in the big luxury flat, in Gezira, which was his home. To him it was a second and much graver warning of his approaching end. For Crash, who had always looked upon his father as being a hale, hearty man, it was a distinct shock. He had had no idea that the old man was so ill; indeed, that he lay under sentence of death. It was more than a grief as well as a surprise to Crash. He loved his father.

For Lucie, it was both pain and sorrow. She went round to the flat every morning to take letters at a dying man's bedside. She liked and respected her employer. He had always been good to her and —he was Crash's father. That, in itself, was enough.

'You've not got to worry, my dear,' Lorrimer said to her one morning, after they had finished their correspondence. She sat looking, sadly, at his grey changed face. 'You're going to be looked after. You needn't think that you'll lose your job when I peg out—I've arranged another one for you.'

'What . . . how . . .?' she stammered, and stopped.

He patted her hand and shook his head mysteriously.

'Wait and see, my child.'

Downstairs in the cool, stone-paved hall of the building, she met Crash. She nearly always met him at this time, coming from a morning's work at Helmieh to see his father. Sometimes she saw that he left Amanda Portlake in the big racing-car which was parked outside the flats. She knew that after he had paid his visit to the old man, he would be off with Amanda for lunch, tea and dinner. And some days he came alone. Today was one of them.

He stopped her in the hall, giving her his friendly, open smile.

'How's Dad and how's little Lucie?'

She answered:

'Your father's about the same. I spoke to the nurse and she said that he is very frail. There isn't a hope, if he gets another of those terrible attacks.'

Crash Lorrimer's handsome face contracted. Lucie was glad to see the contraction. She liked to think that he cared. That vast fortune which was going to be his when old Lorrimer passed over, would be very acceptable. No doubt he would have a grand time on it, but he didn't want to lose the old man.

Said Crash:

'You're looking peeky, my dear. When did you last have any fresh air or exercise?'

A faint colour stole into her cheeks. She tried to laugh.

'Oh, I'm all right.'

He shook his head.

'You never go out. You're always working. If you're not here, you're at the office. You're going back there now, I suppose?'

'After my lunch, yes.'

'Where are you lunching?'

Her colour deepened.

'Oh, somewhere,' she said, evasively.

'Well that "somewhere's" going to be Shepheard's with me. No arguments. I'll meet you at the Grill at half-past one.'

She started to protest. She did not want to go out with Crash. She *did* . . . but it was too much anguish, *afterwards*. She didn't want to suffer again as she had suffered after that dance at the Embassy. Just pure agony, adoring him, wanting him, knowing that he had only the mildest and most platonic interest in her. But Crash did not wait for a refusal. He rushed past her into the lift, and pressed the electric button. As the lift went up, he called through the gates:

'And tell them you won't be back this afternoon. I shall ring up the manager and say Dad wants you.'

44

Lucie walked out of the building and into her employer's car which waited to take her back to Cairo. She felt flustered; a bit dazed. Crash was such a difficult young man to deal with. He just carried one along on the crest of his enthusiasms. Yet why should he worry whether she looked pale, or whether she needed a rest or not. He did not care. He cared for no one except that yellow-haired Amanda—and himself.

'Perhaps,' Lucie thought, bitterly, 'Amanda's out of town again and Crash wants some music.'

She had seen little of him since his father's illness beyond those chance meetings in the hall. But the ache in her heart which was for him only had not diminished one iota.

How depressing it all was! Dear old Mr Lorrimer on his death-bed. She loathed the thought of his going. He had said that she had nothing to worry about. Possibly he had arranged for his manager to keep her on, but it wouldn't be the same without him. And then there was Crash. What in heaven's name would happen to Crash when he was alone in the world, without even the restraining hand of his father who, at least, held the financial reins now!

She felt sudden resentment against Crash because he rushed through life in his joyous irresponsible fashion regardless of anybody else's feelings. Yet *was* he so regardless? He had been awfully kind just now . . . and he was taking her out to lunch.

'*Kind*' . . . the word made her suddenly writhe. She didn't want Crash to be kind. She wouldn't keep that lunch appointment. She hadn't said that she would. He could wait in vain.

But that feeling only lasted with Lucie for a very short time. She was human—and feminine—and she loved Crash Lorrimer.

She met him at Shepheard's at half-past one, glad that she had put on a fresh linen dress this morning. It had a little dark-blue jacket and a pale lemon-coloured scarf which suited her. She never wore a hat but she had taken a lot of trouble at the office combing her glossy brown curls into shape. And she had added an extra bright touch of red to her lips and a faint dusting of rouge-powder on her cheeks because she looked so pale. 'Washed out' was the honest truth.

She had worked hard since Mr Lorrimer's illness, and March had brought warm weather to Cairo. In another few weeks' time, the hot difficult summer would be beginning. Difficult and lonely. No Mr Lorrimer, and that meant—no Crash. For there would be no reason for him to come to the office, nor ring up the Near-East Petroleum Company once his father had gone. The business would be run by one of the junior partners who was shortly coming from London to take over.

Despite the fact that her spirits were low, Lucie appeared to be cheerful enough, during that lunch with Crash.

It was he who was gloomy—very gloomy for him. He was not at all himself.

'Bit of a tragedy, the old boy cracking up at his time of life,' he said, looking at the girl across the table. 'That blasted heart. He ought to have had another twenty years, but for that.'

'If only there was hope!' said Lucie, 'but I'm afraid there isn't.'

'None at all,' said Crash. 'Well, thank God, I shan't have to be long in Cairo after he goes. The regiment goes back to England at the end of the summer.'

Lucie bent over her plate. Into her wide hazel eyes came a look of pain which Crash did not see. Worse and worse . . . the thought of Crash leaving Egypt. Yet wouldn't it be better if she never saw him again? Seeing him hurt so much.

He did a lot of talking. It was as though he liked to confide in her. He was telling her something that his father had said to him today.

'The poor old boy wants me to get married. Thinks I ought to take a wife and settle down, but no thanks!'

Lucie dared to look at him. His gaze was not upon her. A pretty, sleekly turned-out American girl was just passing their table. Crash had caught her eye. He was looking at

47

her with that frank homage which he always had ready for an attractive woman. The American girl gave him a deep side-long glance and a half smile. Lucie thought:

'He knows his power over women . . . he knows how good-looking he is and what a fascination he has for the opposite sex. It is so *bad* for him!'

Yet she could not help feeling glad that he did not want to marry Amanda Portlake.

Crash turned his blue eyes upon her.

'What do you think, little Lucie? Do you think I ought to get myself a fat wife and half-a-dozen screaming children and become a perfect picture of domestic bliss?'

She smiled.

'Why a fat wife—or all those children?'

'God preserve me, really,' he said, laughing. 'I hate fat women. I prefer the children!'

Lucie thanked heaven in that moment for her slenderness. But of course Amanda Portlake was slender, too. How absurd to be jealous of Amanda.

Something, she did not know what, made Lucie say:

'I think Mr Lorrimer wonders if you mean to marry Miss Portlake.'

Crash leant back in his chair and ordered Turkish coffee and cigarettes. He shook his head.

'Not for the moment. If the old man ever says anything to you, you can say I'm not really anxious to marry anybody. Amanda's a lot of fun, but she's an extravagant little brat. She'll want a man with a million.'

He broke off abruptly. Lucie knew that he was remembering the fact that in the near future he would have as much money as Amanda could want. All Lucie's old fears returned. When his father died, he *might* tie himself up to Amanda. And that would be the end of anything fine or good in him. She wouldn't want him to stay in the Army. She'd make him resign and go meandering round the world, spending money and wasting his youth as well as her own.

The subject of Amanda was dropped. Crash turned his attention to Lucie.

'You're a funny little soul! Sometimes you sit so quietly there, like a mouse, watching me with those great eyes. And I wonder what you're thinking.'

She coloured and leaned forward so that he could light her cigarette. His hand almost touched her cheek. Crash had such nice hands, brown and strong yet gentle. The hands of a man who could manage horses—and women!

'I don't suppose I'm thinking about anything much,' she said.

'Nonsense. There are plenty of brains in that small head of yours. In fact, I think you overwork them. A woman shouldn't think too seriously.'

'Then what should she do?'

'Find a man to think for her and give her a good time.'

'I should hate that,' said Lucie abruptly.

'You're a quaint mixture,' said Crash. 'You alternate between Victorianism and modern independence. Most amusing child.'

'I'm glad I amuse you,' she said in the same abrupt voice.

'Well, how about amusing me this afternoon? Come down to the Club. I've got to play one game of squash with a fellow in the XIth and then we'll have tea. Not at the Club. Out at Mena for a change.'

Her heart leapt. That would be fun. To drive in the big, open car out to the Pyramids and have tea at Mena House Hotel. She had never been to the desert with Crash. And the desert was the part of Egypt she loved most. The vastness, the solitude of it, appealed to her. It would be heaven after the dust, the noise of Cairo. The sunset would be wonderful. Sunsets in Egypt never failed to move her. There was something so transcendingly beautiful about the orange and scarlet glow of the sky, with the Great Pyramid towering blackly against it; mighty monument to a dead Pharaoh, belonging to the oldest civilisation in the world. Lucie determined to suffer from no more inhibitions today. Why not live for the moment . . . as Crash, himself, liked to do.

She abandoned the office. Crash had already spoken to the manager. And for the next few hours Lucie was in heaven. While Crash played his game of squash, she sat in the Club and wrote a few letters which she was too tired to do in the evenings. She had an aunt living in Sussex—her mother's sister —and the only relative with whom she kept in close touch. Aunt Milly was a dear and Uncle Rob kept a chicken farm. Lucie had spent a very happy summer there with her father, during the last year of his life. She had been meaning to go back ever since, but had not been able to afford the trip. This summer she must try to afford it. In Aunt Milly's last letter she had said that it was not good for Lucie to be out in Egypt all these years without a break, and it was true. She *was* feeling more and more listless and apathetic as time went on. It would be nice to see England again; the old chicken-farm near the Sussex Downs; a long rest in that lovely garden which was Aunt Milly's joy.

Much as Lucie loved Egypt, while she sat there in the Club today writing home, she had a sudden nostalgia for England. The bright blue sky and the burning sunlight pouring over Gezira vanished. In their place came a vision of the soft mild summer days on Aunt Milly's farm. Of buttercups in green meadows, of trickling brooks, brown woods, blackbirds singing in hawthorn hedges, and little twisting lanes leading toward the gentle green slopes of the Sussex Downs.

Just for a moment, that vision assailed

51

Lucie, but only for a moment. Then returned reality . . . the hard brilliance of this Egyptian day and the torment which was in her heart for Crash.

She sighed and finished her letter and began to wonder whether Crash was not right. He had said that a woman shouldn't think too much. She should find 'a man to think for her and give her a good time'.

Why, why must she give her love where it was not wanted? Lucie asked herself. Why couldn't a girl's pride come to the rescue and save her from the agony of hopeless loving? But it didn't. Pride could save one from an outward betrayal of emotion but never from that pain that goes on deep down in the heart.

It was all a great pity. There was that nice young subaltern in the Sappers who had talked to her just now out on the terrace and asked her to join his felucca party on Saturday night. A crowd of them were going down the Nile for a picnic. Yet she had refused. She knew what it would mean if she went with them. 'A petting party.' There was glamour on the moonlit Nile, drifting in a felucca. She would be thought stupid and unsporting if she objected to a few kisses . . . or her hand being held . . . and she *would* object. She didn't want anybody in the world to touch her, kiss her, except Crash. She felt that she would rather never be kissed again than wipe away the memory of his lips upon hers, that night of the Embassy Ball.

Half an hour later, Lucie was in high spirits again. She had tied a scarf over her curls, and was sitting in the low luxurious seat of Crash's new 'racer', speeding at seventy down the straight Giza road that led from Cairo to the Pyramids.

She could see those tall triangular shapes on the horizon. The desert lay before them. Here and there, a tall date-palm with its green fan of spiky leaves pointing proudly to the sky. Camels padding along the roadside. Black-veiled women with bistred eyes, walking beside little grey donkeys. Those lovely flowering trees that they call golden m'hor; the poignant colour of bougainvillaea, cerise and purple against white walls. The pure desert air blowing against their faces, they rushed toward Mena House. Crash was in much better form after his game of squash. He looked healthy and heart-breakingly handsome, she thought. Grey flannels and striped muffler round his brown throat, his dark hair blowing in the wind. He had to shout at her to make his voice heard above the roar of the engine.

'Goes well, doesn't she?'

'Marvellous!' she shouted back.

Everything was 'marvellous' now. They ate a huge tea in the beautiful gardens of the hotel which lay in the very shadow of the Pyramids. And then, as Lucie had hoped, Crash suggested a walk as far as the Sphinx. She loved the Sphinx. She liked to look at that

53

broken, jagged, inscrutable face and marvel at the age and mystery of it; wonder a little wistfully how many other women, through thousands of years, had stood here, looking at that queer stone beast, half-animal, half-woman, and feel her heart break from unrequited love.

Crash was at his most friendly. Arm tucked through hers, he walked with her a little way in the desert. And as she had hoped, they saw the sunset. The beauty of it caused her intense emotion and she could not speak. She was thankful that he wanted to do all the talking. And after that, it seemed to grow suddenly cold and sombre, so Crash hurried her back to the car, anxious that she should not catch a chill which was so likely in Egypt when the temperature dropped so suddenly.

He tucked a rug around her knees in the car.

'Sure you wouldn't like me to put the hood up?' he asked.

She smiled and shook her head. And her whole body shivered at the touch of his hands.

'I've thoroughly enjoyed my afternoon with you,' he said, and she almost believed him because he spoke so seriously. She answered with apparent nonchalance.

'So have I. It was great fun.'

And not for an instant would she let him dream how much it had meant to her to walk in the desert and watch that sunset beside him.

He had been so very kind, so *sweet* to her. He had not seemed bored. It was difficult to believe that this was the same Crash who was always in hot water; always committing some indiscretion or folly. But no doubt tonight he would be out on another 'blind'. How often she had heard his father speak with dread of Crash driving his car like mad out to some cabaret when he wasn't, perhaps, quite sober. How often she had shared the old man's dread of another, perhaps fatal, accident.

Her heart yearned over him as he drove her back to Cairo. She wondered, sadly, how much more she would see of him except when he passed her in his father's flat. And that wouldn't be much longer since the poor old man hadn't long to live.

Darkness falls rapidly in Egypt where there is no twilight. It was dark by the time Crash pulled the car up outside the Near-East Petroleum Company. Lucie wanted to run into the office to pick up her attaché case which she had left there. It had some work in it which she wanted to do tonight.

'I'll wait for you,' he said, 'and take you home.'

'You needn't,' she began.

'But, of course,' he broke in, and added: 'You know you're a good companion, Lucie. Such a good listener. A fellow can talk to you. I find most women like to do all the talking.'

She did not answer. She was, as always,

55

tongue-tied by his praise. There was some consolation for her in the thought that he liked being with her; that he liked to talk to her about himself. That, coming from Crash, was truly flattering.

She ran up to the office for her case and found a note lying upon it. It had been scribbled by one of the typists.

'In case you come back and don't know— poor old E.L. had a heart attack half-an- hour ago and passed out. We're not to come tomorrow because the office is to be closed.'

Lucie stood still, crumpling the note in her hand. Her face had grown white and grave. She felt a lump in her throat. Poor old Mr Lorrimer. It didn't seem possible! Not possible that he would never come into this office again and look at her with his kindly blinking little eyes; that she would never again go to his bedside with her pad and pencil to take letters; to feel herself again the focus of his friendly attention. She had grown so very fond of him and he had been so kind to her. She felt immeasurably shocked, prepared though she had been for his sudden death.

The tears stung her eyelids and she put up a hand to wipe them away. And then remembered suddenly that Edgar Lorrimer's son was waiting for her downstairs. She would have to tell him. To her must fall the difficult duty of breaking the news to Crash.

Slowly, reluctantly, Lucie picked up her attaché case and went downstairs.

For a moment she stood on the steps of the building, irresolute. Crash was no longer alone in the big blue and silver car. A girl sat beside him. A girl who looked as though she was on her way to a smart party; black dress, silver fox coat, a ridiculous little feathered hat stuck on the side of her platinum fair head. She was laughing up at Crash as Lucie walked toward the car. Amanda! Amanda Portlake, of course.

Crash saw Lucie and, without noticing the change of expression on her face, waved his hand at her.

'Come on, Lucie. Jump in at the back and I'll drive you home.'

She stood still beside the car. In the back, eh? Of course, she must be relegated to the back now that Amanda had come.

'I don't think you two know each other,' went on Crash. 'Amanda, this is Miss Bryant, Dad's secretary. Lucie, my friend, Miss Portlake.'

'How-do-you-do,' said Amanda in a bored voice and with scarcely a glance at the small figure in the shabby Jaegar coat, with the blue scarf over her curls.

'Just met Amanda on her way to the Turf Club,' added Crash. 'I'm going to give her a lift, but we'll take you along to Heliopolis first of all.'

Then Lucie said:

'I'm afraid I've got something I must tell you, Crash.'

He came down from the clouds of flippancy into which Amanda's company always raised him, and stared at Lucie's grave young face.

'Why, what's happened?'

She swallowed hard and suddenly he saw the tears in her eyes. And he knew.

'My father,' he said quickly, 'is it something about him?'

'Yes,' said Lucie, and bowed her head.

Amanda, who had not been paying much attention to what was being said, put in:

'Come on, Crash darling. I'll be late.'

Then he turned to her, all the fun gone out of him.

'I'm sorry, Amanda, I shan't be able to take you to the Club. Do you mind getting a taxi? I must go to Gezira at once. It's the old man . . . Lucie says he's . . . he's passed out.'

Amanda made a suitable show of sympathy. She got out of the car, assuring Crash that she would ring him up at the earliest opportunity. And to herself she was thinking:

'Well, that's the best news I've heard for a long time. Crash will have all the money and no restrictions. *So what? I think* this is where little Amanda gets to work and leads our Crash to the altar!'

In complete silence, Crash opened the car

door for Lucie as though taking it for granted that she would get in and go with him. She knew that he was knocked over by the news. And she slipped an arm through his and held it close to her as they drove together to the flat.

VI

On the day of Edgar Lorrimer's funeral, the offices of the Near-East Petroleum Company were shut. But the holiday was a sorrowful one for Lucie. She missed her kind and considerate employer and the old working days, and she rather dreaded the new life which she presumed she would be leading under the direction of the junior-partner.

Bernard Cadney had flown over to Egypt in time for the funeral and had already introduced himself to Lucie, who was quick to foresee trouble. He was obviously a clever businessman. In the early forties, and with a wife and children whom he had left in London. They were to join him later. But he was the sort of man to be familiar with a pretty typist, and he had more or less hinted to Lucie that they were 'going to get along very nicely'.

'Not as nicely as he imagines,' had been her private comment.

And the knowledge that she would never like Mr Bernard Cadney, nor feel the same interest in her work with him as the 'boss', added to her depression. Life was going to be so grim, so difficult, so *different* without Mr Lorrimer—and Crash!

She did not go to the funeral. Crash would not allow it. But he had telephoned her at the pension to thank her, personally, for her lovely wreath which he knew must have cost half her week's salary. And when she had asked, anxiously, how he was, he had said:

'Oh, bearing up . . . it's all pretty grim . . . of course, I'll be glad when it's over.'

She could imagine how Crash, the gay, easy-going, irresponsible young man must hate all the sombre paraphernalia of death.

Immediately after the funeral he was to see Martin Spenser, his father's solicitor, and read the Will.

More than ever on this gloomy day, Lucie longed to be with Crash—to give him what help and support she could. She hugged to herself the memory of the moment which to her had been such a wonderful one, when she had driven beside him to his father's flat after breaking to him the news of the old man's death. She had felt strangely close to him then. Amanda hadn't counted. It had been just Crash and herself driving together, her arm through his, in silent sympathy.

Last night he had called her up at the pension and asked her to meet him at the Turf Club for a drink at half-past six.

'I daresay there'll be a bit of business to talk

over and I'm quite positive the old man's remembered you in his Will,' he had said. 'He thought a lot of you. Anyhow, let's have a drink together, and you can cheer me up.'

So she had his company to look forward to at the end of the day. But at five o'clock another telephone-call sent her hopes flying to the four winds. Crash cancelled the appointment. Some man—she did not even know who—apologised for him. Mr Lorrimer regretted that he could not meet Miss Bryant as arranged but would get in touch with her later.

After the hours of waiting about, grieving for her lost friend, and full of anxious fears for her future, that cancellation was a blow to Lucie. And still more of a blow when she discovered what she supposed to be the reason for his change of mind.

Young Peter Callow, the Sapper who had for long been trying to induce her to go out with him, suggested that she should drink with him at the Continental and she accepted. She could not face a long, lonely evening—just thinking about Crash.

Walking into the Continental to keep her appointment with Peter, Lucie caught sight of the familiar blue and silver racing-car with Crash at the wheel, heading for the town, and beside him, the equally familiar figure of Amanda Portlake.

Lucie's cheeks burned and she hurried into

61

the hotel with a feeling of intense humiliation. So *that* was why Crash had cancelled his appointment. He did not need her, Lucie, to cheer him. Amanda had come on the scene. Amanda was to be the consoler in her place.

Lucie's brown curly head was tilted high that evening. She was nicer to Peter Callow than she had ever been. She flung herself into the evening's amusement, determined to enjoy it. Accompanied him to a cinema and afterwards to the Kit-Kat cabaret to dance.

'You're in grand form,' Peter informed her and tightened his hold of the small figure while he was dancing with her. She made a gay reply, but looked up into his round, babyish face and thought how completely cold he left her; how utterly unable she was in the depths of her heart to respond to his attentions. It was Crash . . . Crash all the time. The memory of Crash in uniform, dancing with her at the Embassy and of those dizzying moments in his arms. Memories of Crash walking with her in the desert, arm in arm, watching the transformation of the sunset, talking to her in his friendly, confidential way. Why, *why* had he let her down tonight so crudely, so casually, just for the sake of an extra drink with Amanda?

Besides, he had hinted that he would have something to tell her about his father's Will. She would not have been human had she not wondered whether Crash was right and if the dear old man *had* remembered her. And Crash had not even bothered to tell her.

But if Lucie thought that Crash was enjoying his evening with Amanda, she was wrong. He had never enjoyed one less. He was in a white-hot rage . . . almost too angry to speak. In a rage that had consumed him from the moment Martin Spenser had left the Gezira flat, after unfolding to him the contents of the Will. That new Will which apparently had only been made a few weeks before the old man died.

Since five o'clock, Crash and Amanda had been together. Drinking first at one bar, then at another. Crash in his worst mood, his blue handsome eyes blood-shot and furious, his mouth a sullen line.

'I couldn't face Lucie Bryant this evening,' he had said to Amanda when they had first met. 'I just *couldn't* face her. She's a nice enough girl but, my God! Dad's Will is beyond the pale.'

Amanda agreed. Amanda was equally furious. What Crash had imparted to her was the most unattractive news she had heard for some time. It was *damnable*, she thought, for the old boy to have made such conditions. Forcing him into marriage with that twopenny-ha'penny typist! *God*, what a disappointment for *her*, Amanda. After all her plans for securing Crash and his thousands.

'I think Dad must have gone out of his mind

63

to do such a thing,' said Crash, gulping down his drink. 'It's absolutely monstrous. And unfair, which isn't like the old man, either. I always thought he was just.'

Amanda looked at him through her long lashes which were black and glistening and very cunningly curled.

'I can't see his object, can you?'

'Oh, yes,' said Crash, with a short laugh. 'I can see it. He always thought a whole lot of Lucie. Got a bit sentimental about her in the end. Told me once that she reminded him of my mother. No doubt, he imagined she would make me a nice sensible wife who would keep a restraining hand on me and mend me of my evil ways!'

'Dar-*ling*,' cooed Amanda, and pouted her lips which were the same startling scarlet as her long pointed nails. 'I couldn't bear you to be mended of your evil ways. They're such *lovely* ways.'

He gave another laugh and ordered another drink.

'Well, I'm damned if I'm going to be forced into doing anything I don't want.'

'All the same, my sweet,' said Amanda, thoughtfully, 'if you don't do it, you lose a fortune. You'll have about five pounds a week to live on and that means no more Army, no more polo, and, incidentally, no more Amanda!'

Crash, irritable because he was kept waiting

for his drink, clapped his hands and cursed the white-robed *suffragi* who was passing through the lounge of the hotel in which they were now sitting.

'Bring me a gin-and-French and be quick about it.'

To Amanda, he added:

'It looks as though I've got to do without you, anyhow, doesn't it?'

She leaned back in her chair, watching him in that covert way under her sticky lashes. She rather liked Crash when he was a little drunk. He could be so amusing. He was a bit of a bore when he behaved too much like 'an officer and a gentleman' which that pious old father of his had advocated so strongly. As for Lucie Bryant . . . Amanda had only seen her once . . . quite pretty, but middle-class and definitely not up to Crash's standards. He needed something chic and a bit spectacular like himself . . . like *herself.*

She said slowly:

'Now look here, my sweet, it's no good going off the deep-end saying that you won't do this and won't do that. I know you're cross about it. I don't blame you. I expect you feel like smashing everything in Cairo.'

'Yes, everything,' he said, tersely. 'I tell you, Manday, that Will was the most awful shock to me. I took the car and drove down the desert road like hell for an hour after old Spenser told me about it.'

'And you say the girl doesn't know.'

'Apparently not. Spenser says nobody knew about it, except himself.'

'I wonder what the girl will say when she hears.'

'She isn't to know.'

'What do you mean, my sweet? How can she help knowing?'

Crash lit a cigarette. He had been smoking one after the other for the last three or four hours. Those brown slender fingers of his were not quite steady. A black lock of hair fell across his forehead and he did not even bother to push it back. Spoiled all his life, this sudden barrier to everything that he had ever wanted, aroused all that was worst in him. He was infuriated beyond all measure by the mere idea of being forced into matrimony with any woman. It didn't matter whether it was Lucie Bryant or a peeress of the realm. He did not wish to be made to marry any girl except the one he chose for himself. And Lucie Bryant was the very last person in the world that he would have chosen. Pretty, yes. Quite sweet. Nice and friendly to talk to. But to marry . . . good God, no! If there was any girl to whom he would like to find himself tied up, it was Amanda. Manday understood him and his ways.

'One of the stipulations in the Will,' he said, 'is that Lucie shouldn't be told about it. Because obviously if she was told, she wouldn't marry me. She'd know I was only doing it to get the money.'

Amanda sneered.

'Don't tell me she wouldn't marry you whether she knew or not.'

'Well, she wouldn't,' said Crash roughly. 'The old man had her character summed up. She's a queer, reserved sort of child. She'd be horrified at the idea of a fellow marrying her just to get the money, and she'd never do it.'

'Then you've got to tell her you've fallen in love with her, haven't you?'

Through his teeth he said:

'I'm damned if I will.'

Amanda leaned forward and put her hand on his knee, pressing it a little.

'Listen, sweetie, don't go off the deep-end. I'm upset for you, but I'm not going to let you lose your sense of proportion. You know what counts most in this world, don't you? Money! It always has done and always will do. You can't do any of the things you like without it. And I can't see you on five pounds a week, looking for a job. Now, can you?'

He was silent a moment, his dark brows scowling. Then, with a short laugh, he said:

'No, I don't suppose I can.'

'Then you'll have to marry the girl, my pet, *but* there's always a way out a little later on, isn't there?'

He looked at her sulkily.

'You mean marry Lucie and then quit?'

67

'Certainly. I shall be terribly jealous—livid, and all that, but as long as I know you are coming back to me. Well, dar*ling!*'

She looked up at him in her effective way, leaning so close that he could catch the perfume of 'Arpège' from her fair, sleek hair. And he saw her tonight through even rosier spectacles than usual. She was marvellous. Her black dress fitted her perfect figure like a glove. Lanvin dress. Lanvin perfume. And she wore big stud pearls in her ears and dozens of narrow jewelled bracelets.

He could never be bored with her for a moment. If he had to have a wife, he would like Amanda—not Lucie Bryant. He supposed that it wasn't Lucie's fault that all this had happened! Poor kid! But it made him feel resentful against her whether she deserved it or not.

He said:

'My dear Manday, it's all going to be very difficult. The Will says that although no further conditions are to be imposed upon me after marriage when I inherit the money, my father relies on my honour to cherish my wife for the rest of my days.'

Amanda laughed.

'That's absurd, of course. The old man must have been potty. Nobody would blame you for quitting her later on. And not so much later, either!'

'So you say "to hell with honour" and the

rest of it,' said Crash, tensely. 'You think I'd be justified in going through with the marriage and then—coming back to you?'

She whispered:

'If you want to.'

His hand closed over hers and pressed it until she winced.

'You know I do, you little devil. You're the most exciting woman in Egypt.'

'I'll wait for you,' she said. 'Get the marriage over with this wretched girl and just remember . . . I'll be waiting.'

'It's damned decent of you, Amanda,' said Crash huskily. 'After all, you might have walked out on me.'

She said nothing, but she thought:

'Not so long as you're going to get the cash, my sweet. You *and* your fortune are much too devastating. *And* worth waiting for!'

'Mind you,' added Crash, 'I don't know how I'm going through with this thing. It does go against the grain, asking that girl to be my wife, and pretending it's what I want.'

'Try to remember that it's the £. s. d. that you want,' counselled Amanda.

A glimmer of conscience awoke in Crash.

'Is it very fair on Lucie? And why should my father have taken it for granted that she'd accept me, anyhow?'

Amanda gave a scornful laugh.

'Because Mr Lorrimer knew that any girl like Lucie Bryant would fall straight into your arms.'

Crash had a sudden uncomfortable recollection of the night of the Benevolent Ball . . . of a little Victorian figure in pink and silver brocade; of pink roses on brown curls; of a velvety mouth trembling under his kisses. He bit his lips fiercely. She'd accept him if he asked her. Oh yes! That was pretty certain. And the old man must have known it. But it was the devil, the very devil, and grossly unfair upon him. Why have any compunction about marrying Lucie . . . and keeping Amanda in the background until he could get his freedom, and return to her arms.

'Courage, my sweet,' said Amanda. 'Just be philosophical and go through with it. I repeat . . . I'll be waiting.'

He carried her hands to his lips.

'I'm crazy about you, Amanda.'

'And I'm so crazy about you,' she said, 'that I won't let a little frippet like Lucie Bryant part us for more than a very short time. Dar-*ling.*'

'Let's have another drink,' he said roughly, 'then we'll drive out on the desert road and forget our troubles. It will be the last evening of this sort that I can have for some time, if I'm going to propose marriage to Lucie Bryant tomorrow!'

VII

Nobody was more surprised than Lucie when a telephone call from Crash Lorrimer came through for her at the office that next morning.

She was taking letters from Bernard Cadney at the time. Mr Cadney had been prolonging the dictation, enjoying the sight of the slender attractive little figure of his new stenographer. Old Lorrimer had good taste, he told himself. He had been annoying Lucie by becoming personal during business, which was a thing she detested.

'How about a little dinner one evening and a drive to the Pyramids . . .' he had just said.

She refused the invitation politely but firmly. She did not care for Mr Cadney or his ways! She would have liked to have said, straight out:

'You're a married man and just because your wife is three thousand miles away, you can't start this sort of thing with your staff!'

It would have given her a lot of pleasure to make the remark and wipe the self-satisfied smirk from Bernard Cadney's flabby face. But, of course, it would mean wiping her job off the map at the same time and she did not particularly wish to find herself out of work. But if Mr Cadney thought she would visit the Pyramids at night with him, he was mistaken. Once she had wandered out there in the desert with Crash. That memory was going to remain unspoiled.

Then Crash's call . . . awkward for her with Mr Cadney sitting back in his chair, gently beating his finger-tips together, watching her, listening to her. She was conscious of the fact that her cheeks were burning. Crash said:

'Sorry about last night, Lucie. But I want to talk to you sometime. I'm playing polo this afternoon. Can you meet me at the Club for tea, then perhaps we'll fix up something for tonight?'

Her breath quickened with excitement. She bit her lower lip and tried to answer in a stiff little voice—for Mr Cadney's benefit.

'Thank you very much. Yes, thank you . . . I'll be at Gezira Club on the Lida, at half-past four.'

She was glad that Crash did not want to chat over the 'phone in his usual gay fashion. She hated to talk to him in front of Bernard Cadney. No doubt poor old Crash wasn't feeling very gay, after yesterday. But why did he want *her* to go out? Why wasn't Amanda still the consoler? It had been Amanda last night!

She wondered if she ought to be proud and turn down Crash's invitation. But that was stupid. What had pride to do with it? She loved Crash. She had always loved him. If he wanted to take her out, she was going.

The man who had stepped into her old

employer's shoes gave Lucie a sly look over the rim of his glasses.

'Making dates with the boy-friend, eh? But no time for me?'

Her colour was high, but so was her head, when she answered:

'You must forgive me, Mr Cadney. You see I've lived in Cairo some time and I have so many invitations from my old friends.'

'I hope to be placed in that category,' he smiled.

'Mrs Cadney will be over here quite soon, won't she?' smiled Lucie sweetly.

Bernard Cadney cleared his throat and attended to the papers on his desk.

'Quite so. Quite so!'

But he registered a vow to get even with Miss Bryant for *that*. Changing his tone, he said:

'There'll be a lot of work this afternoon and I doubt if you will be away by half-past four. Are you in the habit of going off early?'

For a moment she did not answer. She thought:

'How well you live up to the first three letters of your name . . .'

And it seemed to her a pity that Edgar Lorrimer's partner should be a man of this quality. But even for Crash she was not going to be accused of neglecting her duty.

'If I had got through my letters, Mr Lorrimer never minded me leaving at tea-time,' she said. 'It gets pretty hot here during the afternoon later on this month. Then of course we do not open until four and I work until seven. But if you will tell me what time I shall be away, I'll let Mr Lorrimer know.'

That name made Bernard Cadney sit up. Young Lorrimer, eh? So that was the boy-friend! Well, of course, that made things a bit different. Young Lorrimer would soon be in control of a great deal of the money in the firm.

Mr Cadney murmured:

'Ah, well, I've no doubt you'll be through by half-past four. Now would you kindly take this letter.'

Lucie bent over her pad, smiling.

Going down to Gezira Club later on that day, she felt suddenly more cheerful than she had been since poor old Mr Lorrimer's death. Nothing could get her down if Crash wanted to see her. Not even working for that hateful man. She was glad that she had mentioned Crash's name to him. That had made him alter his tone. But it was plain to be seen that her pathway at the office would not in future be as easy as it had been in old Lorrimer's life-time.

She waited at the little table on the terrace facing the Club swimming pool, until Crash came. He walked out of the changing-room, looking hot and sunburnt after his game of polo. It gave her a heartache to see him. Crash, 'the Magnificent'. There wasn't a man amongst all these Army officers sitting around to touch him. He greeted her with his old flippancy.

'How's little Miss Victoria? Sorry if I've kept you waiting. Phew! it's hot. We had a good game but my pony went lame in that last chukka. Damned nuisance. The Gunners won.'

'I'm sorry about that,' said Lucie.

He clapped his hands and ordered tea. A white gowned Egyptian with a red-tasselled tarboosh on his black head came up with a tray of cakes.

'What will you eat?' asked Crash. 'Choose one of these creamy, sticky things. I'm going to have toast.'

Lucie, being young and hungry, took a chocolate cake and was at once the envy of the women sitting nearby who were fatter than Lucie and on slimming diets.

Crash looked at Lucie and for a moment ceased his cheerful banter and reminded himself that this was the girl whom he was being forced to marry. *Marry!* The very word put the wind up him, he thought. Yet she was a charming little thing. Of course, she hadn't Amanda's chic or poise, neither had she got that 'snap' in her which Amanda possessed. Amanda was always at the top of her form, with her aptitude for drinks and racy stories and her amazing flow of American wise-cracks which made him laugh.

But Lucie was pretty, and had good taste.

He liked that blue linen dress with its short sleeves showing rounded sun-browned arms. Her curls had the gloss of horse-chestnuts in the sun. And her eyes were so very soft and adoring. Yes, there was no doubt that Lucie adored him. Lucie was his for the asking. And the old man had known that, *blast it.* His grief for the loss of his father had been very much tempered by bitter resentment, since he had read the Will.

'How are things, Crash?' Lucie was asking.

'Okay,' he said briefly.

She looked critically at the lines around his eyes. Such restless, handsome eyes. And that slim brown hand lifting the tea-cup to his lips was never quite steady. Too many drinks, too many cigarettes, too many late nights.

'You never give yourself any rest, do you?' she smiled at him.

'Who wants rest?' he said and laughed with a flash of his old spirit. 'When one's dead, my dear Lucie, one will rest for a long long time. Make the most of life while you can, is my motto.'

Lucie sighed.

'I suppose so.'

He felt suddenly curious to know what lay at the back of her mind.

'What do you ask of life, anyhow?'

Lucie looked down at the cake which she was cutting with a fork.

'Oh—lots of things.'

'For instance?'

'A trip to England this summer. The English countryside in June. The Sussex Downs.'

'H'm,' said Crash, 'your desires are modest, my child.'

And he thought, cynically, of the difference in women. Once he had asked Amanda what she wanted of life and she had said:

'You . . . a yacht . . . Monte Carlo . . . the world . . .'

'I know the Sussex Downs,' he said. 'They're pretty good. I was at prep-school in Brighton, and I used to ride over the Dyke. But I haven't been there for years.'

'I hope to take my holiday this June, if I can afford it,' she said.

He felt a sudden desire to be brutal. To say:

'You wait, my child. No Sussex Downs for you. You'll come with me when I go home on leave, and beat up London, Paris and New York, whether you want to or not. That's what you'll have to do when you are my wife. I'll need plenty to distract me if I've got to be your husband.'

But of course she didn't know yet that she was going to marry him, poor little Lucie. Amanda might envy her. He didn't. He had no illusions about himself. He felt rotten . . . rotten to the core because he was going to carry out his father's wishes for such an ignoble reason . . . to get money . . . nothing else . . . quite regardless of this girl's personal

77

happiness.

He said:

'I told you my father might remember you in his Will. But he didn't exactly leave you any money.'

The colour sprang to her cheeks.

'Oh, Crash, but of course not . . . I mean . . .'

'Never mind about that,' carried on Crash hurriedly. 'I'll see you get all the holiday you want this year.'

Embarrassed she said:

'That's all right.'

He finished his toast and lit a cigarette.

'You've worked rather hard all your young life, haven't you?'

'Since Daddy died, yes.'

'Hard work and loneliness. Not the right diet for a young and attractive girl.'

She thrilled to the word 'attractive'. Did he really find her so? Laughing, she said:

'Oh, I've done very well on it. I seem to be better than a lot of girls who do nothing and are always getting ill.'

He looked at the pink of her cheeks and the starry brightness of her eyes. Amanda had to get that sort of colour out of a pot. He knew it. Why the hell he was so crazy about Amanda, he couldn't think. Why couldn't he get the same 'kick' out of a girl like Lucie who was fresh and natural and innately *good*.

Last night he had felt nothing but impotent fury and a bitterness against Lucie which she did not deserve. He had dreaded meeting her to-day. Dreaded what he must do. But he had to admit that when he was with her, he felt curiously at peace. She had a soothing effect upon him. And the very fact that she worked so hard, and asked for so little, made him a bit ashamed of himself. It was with a genuine desire to give her happiness that he issued an invitation for this evening.

'We'll dine and dance—shall we? Get on a pretty dress, and I'll take you to the Continental Cabaret. Dad particularly wished that I shouldn't make any show of mourning. At least, that I was not to sit down, and refuse to go out. So we'll dance, shall we? Would you like it?'

'I'd just love it, Crash,' she answered, and hoped that he did not guess just how much she *would* love that outing.

They walked into the Club together after tea. Everybody knew Crash; nodded, smiled or said a few words. And several people knew Lucie and waved to her. She was frightfully proud because she was with Crash.

He drove her back to Heliopolis and left her to change. With dancing heart, she ran her bath and tipped in all the gardenia bath-salts which she had left over from a Christmas present with which she had been very sparing. She would use it all tonight. *Tonight* she was going to dance with Crash again. It would be like the Embassy Ball. Oh, so delirious, dancing with Crash. She was madly happy because he wanted her companionship. What did work matter, money or the lack of it? What did that horrid old Mr. Cadney matter? Nothing did! *Nobody* did! She was going out with Crash and the world seemed a radiant place to live in.

She only had one evening-dress except that rose brocade. The inevitable black. A year old. But it looked quite nice and she hoped and believed that Crash would like it. It was black net with a wide skirt which had narrow black velvet bands. Black velvet straps over her shoulders; a little net coat with a Peter Pan collar, and short puff sleeves. There was a big bunch of artificial violets pinned to one shoulder. And she wore her pearls, and Mummy's bracelet. Nothing to choose from; always the same things. But perhaps Crash would not bother about that.

There was nothing of the tired office girl about Lucie when Crash picked her up at the pension in his car. He had put up the hood and side-curtains in order to protect her from the night air. Thoughtful of him. He was really a dear and so terribly generous, she told herself. Looking superb as usual, in his dinner-jacket . . . . carnation in his button-hole, dark hair smoothly brushed . . . brown face newly shaven . . . white silk muffler round his throat. Crash, the irresistible, the most debonair young man in Egypt. And she, Lucie, was going out with him. Lucky Lucie! If only she had a decent coat, she sighed. She had never been able to afford furs. Only that little dyed rabbit-cape . . . white . . . *not* so white after two years in Egypt . . . and getting a yellowish tint from being cleaned so much.

But Crash had a flattering word for her. 'You look sweet,' he said.

That was enough for her. She sat at his side driving down to Cairo, feeling that life could hold no more for her than this.

Crash started out by being bored. Amanda had called him up at the Mess just before he changed.

'I'm so jealous of that beastly little typist,' she had said. 'I can hardly bear it. Oh, I know you've got to go through with it, but meet me tomorrow sometime. You needn't let her know it. You've got to meet me often. We'll both pass out if we don't see each other.'

He had agreed, sympathised with her, pitied himself. He would meet her and drive her out of Cairo somewhere tomorrow afternoon.

But he wasn't so bored with Lucie as the evening went on. There was no use denying the fact that she was a good companion. She came out of her shell, and proved that she could be quite amusing. And she danced like a dream. Better than Amanda. There was no denying *that* fact. No partner he had ever had melted into his arms quite like Lucie. She was sweet and fragrant to hold and there was something appealing about her smallness. She must have tiny bones, he thought. Tiny little wrists and ankles, and that curly brown head only just reached his cheeks. Amanda was a good deal taller. Amanda was so much more sophisticated. Lucie was a mere kid, really, but an awfully nice kid, he thought. And she did enjoy herself so thoroughly. She didn't grumble like Amanda about the band, the drinks, the other people. Amanda, at times, could be very *exigeant* . . . difficult. But everything was good to Lucie. A fellow couldn't be bored, seeing a girl like that enjoy herself so completely.

He discovered tonight that she had a 'voice'. An attractive way of crooning in a husky little voice. She knew all the words of the dance tunes and he made her sing them while they danced.

'Where did you get that talent from?' he teased her. 'You oughtn't to be in an office. You ought to be at the B.B.C., charming millions of listeners.'

She laughed:

'Here's an old one . . .' and crooned the words as they moved across the dance floor to the lilt of a waltz, in perfect accord with him.

'I give my heart just to one man
Loving as only woman can.
This too I swear, while I am there
All I possess is his to share . . .'

Crash shook his head at her, and gave a smile, slightly derisive.

'That's a lot of nonsense, isn't it? Women don't love men that way!'

'Of course they do,' said Lucie, indignantly.

'I've never met one.'

'You're a horrid old cynic, Crash.'

'Horrid, I agree.'

She laughed up at him, her cheeks aglow.

'Well, you don't know anything about *how* women love . . . when they do.'

'And what do you know about it?' he jeered.

She swallowed hard and shook her head.

'Nothing!'

'Then it's time you learned,' he said.

She was speechless. Of course he was just fooling about . . . Crash in one of his gay, inconsequent moods. Well, it was so very lovely while it lasted. Let him carry on . . . she didn't care . . . she must school her emotions and be mistress of her own heart, and not allow him to break it.

He was in much higher spirits when they left the cabaret than when they had entered it. There was something almost reckless about him tonight which she did not quite understand. Almost as though he was *determined* to enjoy himself and make her the focus of his attention. He flattered her unduly. Their dancing had been grand . . . her crooning had made it perfect . . . he saw no

83

reason why they shouldn't dine and dance much more often . . . and the next time he would see that she had real violets to wear. Violets were obviously her flowers, he said. They ought to be wood-violets. She was like a wood nymph with her hazel eyes and her chestnut curls. And the cherry blossom of her cheeks.

He did not drive her straight home. He took her through Heliopolis and out to the desert. Lucie was carried along on the crest of his enthusiasm, dazed by his admiration, half inclined to believe that he really did like taking her out.

And what a night! A new moon, a slender silver crescent on a great black disc which seemed to hang in a sky glittering with stars. It was calm and quiet out here and the night air was cool and fresh after the over-heated, smoky atmosphere of hotels.

When Crash stopped the car and switched off the engine, there was not a sound to be heard, except the distant yapping of the pie-dogs—those lonely scavengers of the East.

In the dim blue dusk, Lucie could just see her companion's face, that handsome arrogant young face. All the arrogance was wiped from it now. In this light he looked tired and even sad. And suddenly, wordlessly, he turned and gathered her into his arms.

She felt as though she was dying . . . that she could not breathe, so intense was the feeling he roused in her. His arms were demanding and the pressure of his lips subtle and slow, draining the blood from her heart.

He kissed her more passionately than he had done on the night of the ball. Loving him as she did, she could not begin to analyse his reasons for making love to her like this. He did not love her, she knew that. He had not loved her when he had kissed her the other night, and she had suffered for it, afterwards. She was a fool to let him kiss her now, knowing that she would suffer again. Yet it was beyond her power to resist.

But at last, those kisses grew too intense and she could no longer bear them. She put up a hand and put it across his mouth. She whispered:

'Crash . . . don't . . . please!'

'Why not?' he said, almost harshly.

He kept his arms about her. One of his hands played with her curls. (She had an insane desire to catch hold of that hand and put it against her cheek.) And he was thinking:

'What a brute I am! I'm in love with Amanda and I'm making love to this child as though *she* was the woman in my life. Well, damn it, it's my father's fault. I've no other choice. And if she wants to return my kisses . . .'

He repeated:

'Why not? Don't you like me to kiss you, Lucie?'

She sat silent a moment. He could feel her small body trembling in the curve of his arm. A sudden feeling of pity for her swept over him. He picked up her hands, crushing them together in one of his, and kissed the tips of her fingers.

'My sweet,' he said, 'you needn't be frightened of me, you know.'

She was not afraid of him—but of herself. Afraid because the blood rushed so wildly through her veins and because it was so difficult to control the emotion he roused in her.

'Crash, you fool, why don't you see that I'm hopelessly in love with you,' she cried within her.

But he went on telling her not to be frightened and that he would always look after her. Well, what did he mean by that? Perhaps he was just intoxicated by the moonlight and the desert and the fact that they had danced so well together.

Gently, she tried to extricate herself from his arms.

'Let me go . . . dear . . . please!'

But he pulled her back against him, and his lips sought hers again. Between the slow deep kisses he murmured:

'Little Lucie . . . you're like a little bird trembling in my hands . . . darling, you're so young . . . such a child. I'm terribly fond of you, Lucie.'

Her heart ached until she could scarcely bear it. Was he really fond of her? Was that true? She knew Egypt, and the glamour of these desert nights. She did not blind herself to the fact that a man could lose his head very easily in circumstances like these, and she would be mad to believe a single word Crash Lorrimer said to her. Crash . . . whose real girlfriend was Amanda.

Determinedly she pushed him away.

'Really . . . you mustn't . . . kiss me any more!'

'Don't you like me a little bit?'

'You know that I do,' she said, breathlessly. He dropped a last kiss on her curls.

Gloomily he thought:

'There's something about this girl that makes me feel a rotten cad. I can't ask her to marry me tonight. I can't. It's too soon, anyhow. She won't believe in me if I rush things.'

He straightened his tie, smoothed back his hair and pulled a cigarette-case from his pocket.

'Let's smoke, darling,' he said.

The 'darling' came so naturally from his lips that it almost broke her heart. She was still dazed from his kisses. She could only sit there and try to pull herself together and think how wonderful it would be to be really loved by Crash.

But she took her cue from him, smoked and

talked in a practical strain . . . just as though there had never been an embrace between them. Later, when he turned the car round and headed for her pension, her heart sank lower. She thought:

'My evening's over . . . tomorrow it will be Amanda again.'

But to her intense surprise, before he left her, he made her promise to go out with him again that next night.

'There's a new flick coming . . . a good one . . . I'll get seats for it, then we'll dance again.'

She was standing by the car saying goodnight to him when he made that invitation. Her heart beat fast but she looked at him doubtfully.

'It's very good of you, Crash . . . but . . . isn't there someone else you'd rather take out . . . and . . .'

'No, I want to take you out,' he interrupted, almost curtly. 'So-long. Goodnight, Lucie. Tomorrow . . . Turf Club, seven o'clock.'

The big racing-car roared down the moonlit road. Lucie stood staring after it, her thoughts in a jumble, one hand to her throat. He *was* queer. She didn't understand him. And *what* about Amanda?

Well, why worry if Crash wanted to take her out again? Another evening with him . . . more dancing . . . yes, but no more kisses. Oh, no! She couldn't bear that. It wasn't fair.

She let herself into the pension, alternating

between ecstasy and sorrow . . . Only one clear thought in her head. She loved Crash better than life itself. And whatever he might say in his cynicism about women, she would give her heart 'just to one man' . . . for always . . . no matter what came of it.

VIII

Crash Lorrimer took Amanda for that run down the desert road as he had promised. But curiously enough he did not enjoy it. He told himself that he was just worried and harassed about the whole affair of marrying a girl against his own inclinations. Amanda said that he wasn't in 'good form'. Well . . . he wasn't! When they pulled up at a favourite place of theirs to smoke, and exchange an embrace, he found himself enjoying the cigarette more than the kisses.

Amanda's lips were as responsive as ever— even more so. She seemed unusually fervent in the way she clung to him. And of course, he told himself, he was crazy about her. She looked a dream. It was a hot day, and she was all in white, with a big floppy panama hat on the side of her platinum fair head. Around her slender waist, she wore an amusing white suede belt on which the words: 'LONDON . . . PARIS . . . NEW YORK' stood out in gilt letters.

Her long lovely legs were stockingless and her sandal shoes showed the scarlet varnish of toe-nails which matched the tips of her thin fingers. Amanda was so much taller than Lucie, he thought. Thinner, more brittle, somehow; less round and small and sweet. Amanda went to a fellow's head like wine. Lucie was spring water, cool, clear and comforting.

Curious, how he found himself comparing the two girls this afternoon. He had never done that before. He had never before imagined they could ever bear comparison. Amanda was so much more 'his type' in every way. And yet . . . while he sat there, exchanging wise-cracks with her, he was no more excited or satisfied than he had been with Lucie yesterday.

He failed to understand himself and did not try. In consequence he was irritable. His nerves felt all jagged. He did not tell Amanda how marvellous she was, quite as many times as she liked him to, so she, too, became irritable.

'Just because you've got to marry this miserable typist, I don't see why you should spoil our moments together,' she complained.

He apologised briefly and tried to be more amusing. But in a strange way he was annoyed, because Amanda spoke disparagingly of Lucie. He didn't love Lucie, but, damn it all, it wasn't her fault that he had to marry her. She was always very decent to him, and she was not a 'miserable typist'.

When he parted from Amanda, he tried to get back the old feeling of gaiety and pleasure in her company.

'Sorry I've been a bore,' he said, 'just a bit off colour, Honey-head.'

She smiled at him through her long lashes, pleased to hear the nickname he had given her.

'Go and propose to Lucie Locket, or whatever her name is, and get it over,' she said, her red lips pouting at him, 'the sooner you're married and in possession of the dough, the better, Big Boy. I'll be waiting. Don't forget.'

'I'll never forget,' he said, kissed her hand and told himself he certainly couldn't live without her. Amanda was a necessary stimulant—like alcohol. It was just an 'off day' for him, as he had told her.

But he did not care for what he had to do tonight. He was furiously angry with his father for making that Will. He did not want to marry Lucie. But he wanted the money. Be damned if he would live on two hundred and fifty a year, send in his papers and sell those corking polo ponies which he had bought this season. No . . . not if he could keep everything by marrying the girl of his father's choice.

But he still had a conscience. He was

brought face to face with that fact when he met little Lucie this evening. He had a conscience, and it worked as soon as he was with her. Somehow it seemed such a dirty trick to make her think that he cared for her. She was such a darling, really. And that undisguised adoration in those golden hazel eyes of hers was enough to make a fellow feel a cur.

He was just about as silent and moody in Lucie's presence as he had been in Amanda's. He was glad that they did not have to talk during the cinema. But afterwards when they were having supper and dancing, he had to remember the task he had set himself. He tried to be extra attentive to Lucie. He had remembered to send her violets this evening. She had thanked him for them, starry-eyed, and wore them pinned to the black net dress.

'I've only got one dress,' she laughingly told him, 'except the ball-dress, and I can't wear that at this sort of show. You see, I'm not used to all this going-out, so you'll have to forgive me.'

He assured her that she looked charming and was suddenly pleased because at least, he told himself, he could buy her a couple of dozen evening dresses—or more, if she wanted them—once she was his wife.

Lucie noticed his unusual demeanour. She had not seen him look so glum or so preoccupied since his father's death.

'What's worrying you?' she asked him. He said:

'Nothing—why do you ask?'

Her grave eyes regarded him anxiously.

'I don't know. You look . . . you don't look yourself. You look as though you have something on your mind.'

That gave him an opening. He seized it. And yet hated himself even as he said the words because he knew they betrayed her trust in him.

'I *have* got something on my mind,' he said. '*You!*'

At the same time his hand closed over hers and pressed it hard against his knee. Lucie was staggered. Not so much by that gesture as by the way he said that word . . . '*You*'. It both astonished and excited her.

They were sitting at a sofa-table in a secluded corner of the dance-room. The cabaret was on and the lights were lowered. But Crash was not paying any attention to the exhibition-dancers who were whirling in the limelight before him. He was looking at Lucie. Her heart almost stopped beating because he looked down at her like that out of the corner of his blue, attractive eyes.

She managed to find her voice.

'What about—me?'

'Can't you guess?' he asked her.

Again she was staggered. She had no idea what was coming next. He felt her fingers quiver in his and loathed himself. It was all very well for Amanda to say . . . 'Marry the girl and get it over . . .' but it wasn't going to be so easy as that.

Lucie's answer was low and hesitant.

'I can't guess.'

'I won't tell you here,' he said. 'Let's go.'

She was reduced to complete silence. What Crash had in his mind she could not, dared not think. Of course she was mad, she told herself. Any other boy-friend who spoke to her like that . . . well, she would know what was coming next. She would take it for granted that she was about to receive a proposal, or at least a confession of love. But it couldn't be that with Crash . . . it *couldn't*.

He looked down at her face as they walked out of the building into the starlit night and saw that it was pale and tense. He thought:

'I can't go through with it . . . it isn't fair . . . she's too nice.'

He had not brought his own car tonight. He had hired a limousine with a driver. He told the man to drive slowly out of Cairo on to the desert road. (Damn that desert road and memories of Amanda, this morning!) The whole thing was monstrous. To behave like this between two women . . . Beastly . . . dishonest . . . and yet, his father had asked for it. What else could a fellow do when he was faced either with marrying the woman chosen for him, or becoming something next door to a pauper.

Once in the limousine, he had a mental picture of all that he would lose if he lost his father's fortune. Amanda, of course. His commission . . . (he loved the Army). And the polo. God, he couldn't sell those ponies, and never feel quite the thrill of thudding across the polo-ground after that little white ball.

He heard Lucie's soft voice:

'I wish you'd tell me what's wrong, Crash. You look ill. Not yourself. Can't I help? You know I'll always be your friend if you want one . . .'

He said hoarsely:

'Perhaps I want more than friendship from you, Lucie.'

Silence. She could not speak for a moment, but she held herself very tense and still and the little pulse in her throat beat crazily. Then she managed to say:

'Crash, what do you mean?'

He turned and looked down at her. There was a queer appeal in his eyes which she could not see. It might have been an appeal for forgiveness, for understanding. But she did not know. She was conscious only of the fact that his arms were around her and that he was crushing the violets against her breast until the perfume arose from the bruised petals like incense between them. Then the words tumbled from his lips, hotly, disjointedly.

'I want you to marry me, Lucie. Help me

that way, my dear. I need you for my wife. I think I've always needed you. Since my father's death I've realised it . . .' the words seemed to stick in his throat, but he went on. 'Will you marry me, Lucie? Do you love me? Will you marry me . . . answer, please.'

A queer, rough proposal. Not at all like the slick laughing Crash who found it so easy to make love to pretty women when they were in his arms. But this girl in his arms tonight noticed nothing amiss about it, and mistook that roughness for intensity of feeling. For why should he ask her to marry him unless he meant that he wanted her for his wife?

It took her a little time to gather herself together and reply. She knew that she loved him better than anybody on earth. But it was all such a shock . . . Crash wanting to marry her . . . 'needing her'. . . that's what he said. He had always *needed* her. Oh, it was sweet, too sweet to know . . . almost unbearably so.

She gave a little broken cry, and one small hand crept up and trembled against his head, pulling it down to hers.

'I don't quite understand why you should love me, Crash,' she whispered. 'It's all too wonderful. I never dreamed of this. But I do love you. I've never loved anybody else and never will.'

He drew a deep breath and tightened his clasp of her. But for a moment he did not touch her lips. He buried his face against the warm softness of her neck. He was glad that she could not see the sick and ashamed look in his eyes. He had won . . . won easily. Without a fight. Just as his father had known he would win. The money was his . . . and all that it entailed. But the simple and frank declaration of love from this child was more than he had bargained for. It made him feel a cheat . . . and something worse.

Then he told himself that he was a fool. After all, he was only doing what his father had wanted. What Lucie wanted, if it came to that. Why worry? Why let conscience be a torment to him now?

He took fire from the sweetness of Lucie's soft young body trembling in his arms. She was like a bird he had told her the other day . . . a scared bird in a boy's hot hand. He was seized with the sudden overwhelming desire to make her happy, and never to let her guess what lay at the back of this proposal, tonight.

'Lucie,' he whispered huskily, 'darling little thing . . .'

And then it was so easy for that kiss which he laid upon her upturned mouth to be long and passionate, and all that a woman desired. And when he said at the end of that kiss: 'I love you,' he almost meant it. And in Lucie's dizzy brain and enraptured heart there rang the memory of immortal words which she had once heard spoken in *Romeo and Juliet*. She whispered them, eyes shut, pulses shaken with the wonder of this miracle which had happened to her.

'*Now, I defy you, stars!*'

IX

A while later, Crash told the chauffeur to stop the car and wait. He walked with Lucie off the road and with an arm about her, led her on to the top of a sandy hill from which they could see an immeasurable distance.

She stood there in the curve of that strong arm, almost too happy to breathe. She looked, as he bade her, at the twinkling lights of Cairo and Heliopolis and out beyond the Pyramids. He said:

'I always like this view. I often come out here and look at it. There is magic in the desert, Lucie, and the lights of that city which was built here so many thousands of years ago.'

The cool night wind of the desert blew upon their faces. Above them the stars were cold and glittering and very large. Suddenly Lucie flung her arms above her head with a gesture of utter rapture.

'Oh!' she said, 'oh, Crash, what a wonderful, wonderful world!'

He moved his arm and looked at her. The delicate fabric of her skirt was blown about her knees and moulded to her figure. She looked, he thought, almost ethereal, like a little statue of ecstasy in the moonlight. The same feeling of shame smote him which he had felt when she had first told him that she loved him. He wished that she didn't—that she was marrying him just for his money. Anything except for love. For what right had he to her heart's devotion?

He had a quick vision of Amanda, fair, sleek, sneering a little at him.

'You can't take it,' she would jeer, 'you're *yaller* . . .'

He turned abruptly from the sight of Lucie's rapturous face and figure.

'Come, let's go back,' he said abruptly.

Lucie came down from the heights. She was suddenly conscious of a change in him. His handsome face was stern. She gave a little sigh and said:

'Crash, do you *really* want to marry me?'

'Yes,' he said, in the same abrupt voice.

'I hope I shan't bore you. I'm not terribly amusing.'

'You're all right,' he said, with a half-laugh.

'I'm very lucky,' she said, with a catch in her voice, and slipped a small confiding hand through his arm.

'No, I'm the lucky one, Lucie.'

'I think,' she added softly, 'that Mr Lorrimer would have been glad.'

Crash swallowed hard.

'I'm sure of that,' he said, with a bitterness which Lucie did not detect.

They started to walk back to the road. Lucie turned her heel in the soft sand and gave a little exclamation:

'I haven't exactly got the sort of shoes for the desert.'

Immediately he picked her up in his arms and insisted upon carrying her back to the car.

'You're like a kid,' he said, 'you're so small and light. You'll have to eat more. You're too thin. And you'll have to stop work, too, right away and start to enjoy life for a bit.'

Her hands were locked about his neck, her curly head rested against his shoulder. She thought:

'It's much, much too good to be true. I feel as though I'm in a dream. Only please, God, never let me wake up!'

When they were in the car driving back to the city, Crash talked and smoked a lot. He held one of her hands but did not seem inclined for any more emotional scenes. The one wish at the back of his head was to be alone. The hot gust of passion that had shaken him when he had first tasted the sweetness of Lucie's young, responsive lips, had passed, leaving him disgusted with himself. If he must do this thing, then he must do it, he thought, but with as little hypocrisy as possible. He would try not to tell this child again that he loved her. She was too nice for such lies. One

100

day he meant to leave her and he knew it. And if he intended to play a dirty trick like this, he had better not fill her up with too many ideas of what *he* felt about her. Better just to make her as happy as possible while they were together and leave it at that.

He had plans for her and he was masterful about them. Lucie said she would be only too glad to go on working at the office. But he would have none of it. She was to tell Mr Cadney tomorrow morning that she would be leaving at once. She was to move, too, from her cheap 'digs' to the Heliopolis Palace Hotel. He would get her a suite there. He wanted her to live in comfort and to have everything that she needed.

She gasped as she listened to him.

'But, Crash . . .'

'No arguments,' he said, 'my father would like you to have what you want, and I'm here to see to it.'

(That was half true. At least he could feel sincere and be sincere about treating Lucie handsomely and saying that it was 'his father's desire'.)

Finally Crash said:

'We won't have a long engagement. Let's get married quite soon. I'll see my Colonel about it. One has to get permission when one is a subaltern, you know. But, of course, he won't object.'

She was speechless. Her small fingers clung

convulsively to his hand. She felt quite helpless. It certainly wasn't much good arguing with Crash. And he seemed to have everything quite firmly arranged in his mind. Well . . . everything he wanted, she wanted too. And, of course, it would be marvellous to know that she needn't work any more . . . and to live in a lovely hotel.

Just before they reached Heliopolis, she said:

'Crash, what made you fall in love with me? I've always adored you, you know, but I didn't think it was me you loved. I thought it was . . . Amanda Portlake.'

He dropped her hand. His cheeks were red. He said:

'I'm going to marry *you*, Lucie.'

The query he had dreaded but which was so natural, came from her:

'Do you really love me?'

'Yes,' he said, and added to himself: 'God forgive me.'

His goodnight kiss was as long, as fervent as she wished. In a queer way he felt that he owed it to her to make her happy *now*, whatever he did in the future. But he was bitterly ashamed of himself when she seized his hand, pressed it against her hot, young cheek and whispered:

'I do so adore you, Crash . . .'

He went back to the garrison, wondering whether the game was worth the candle. He would save his fortune for himself by marrying Lucie, and afterwards he would gain the woman whom he had always found so fascinating, so amusing, so much his type. But he had not really bargained for the embarrassment that Lucie caused him by her unaffected and simple worship of himself. It made him feel the lowest type of blackguard.

That night, which marked Lucie's engagement to Crash and which for her was the happiest of her life was, for him, one of the most miserable.

From that night onward, Lucie's existence seemed to change miraculously for the better. She went to bed in a state of complete jubilation. She woke with the same grand and glorious feeling. She was to meet Crash for lunch and then go with him to buy her engagement-ring. Her very throat seemed to throb with happiness at the thought. And she had to admit it was pretty good to be able to go into Bernard Cadney's room, hand in her resignation and explain why. She felt a very human pride when she saw the look of astonishment on his face alter to one of deference.

'You're going to marry Mr Lorrimer? Indeed, *indeed* let me congratulate you, Miss Bryant.'

Of course, other congratulations were showered upon her by the rest of the staff. One of the girls who had worked with her, said, enviously:

'My God, you're lucky! He's wickedly attractive. And all that cash . . .'

'I don't mind about the cash,' said Lucie, 'but I'm very much in love with him and I admit it.'

She was still more in love when the end of the day found her with a very lovely ring on her engagement finger. Crash made her choose it for herself and approved. It was a ring she had seen many times in the case of the jeweller's shop just inside Shepheard's Hotel. It was not a modern ring, but a curious little circlet of twisted gold in which was set a variety of lovely stones, rubies, emeralds, yellow diamonds. Inside was an Arabic inscription which, the jeweller told her, meant *'Thou hast my heart'*. And there was a history around that ring. It had belonged to an Egyptian princess and been rifled at some time from her tomb in the Valley of Dead Kings, which was in Upper Egypt. It was the betrothal ring of the princess. At the age of sixteen years she had married a prince of royal blood, whom she loved devotedly. After two years of married happiness, the young pair had died together in a plague. A tragic story, but Lucie was not superstitious. The romance of the ring appealed to her and she refused to have an expensive modern jewel. She said to Crash:

'*"Thou hast my heart"*, and we shall prove ourselves a happy pair, even though not of royal blood. And it is to be hoped that we shall live many years so that the spirit of the little princess will see us together and be glad that I have her ring.'

Crash was embarrassed. He was so used to sarcasm and 'wise-cracks' from Amanda, he was nonplussed by Lucie's sentiments. He laughed and called her a 'romantic child'. But he told her that the little Egyptian ring looked charming on her sun-browned hand.

'Such a small hand, too,' he said. 'You must be about the same size as the princess.'

She was with him all the afternoon. But he had an appointment which he could not break that evening, he told her, apologetically. She said:

'Why, of course, you mustn't bother about me. There'll be all sorts of evenings when you have to dine in Mess, and that sort of thing, won't there?'

But Crash wasn't dining in Mess. He was seeing Amanda. Amanda who had rung him up at Helmieh and intimated that she felt a bit neglected. But Lucie wouldn't know. And he tried to deceive himself into believing that he really needed Amanda's company. She was of his own calibre. He could be cynical with her. He could kiss her, hold her, without that feeling of shame which smote him every time he took Lucie in his arms.

Amanda was subtle that evening. She saw at once the state of mind which Crash was in. She knew that he was not liking his job, as Lucie's fiancé. He had too much of a conscience. She made no complaints about her own lot. She saw to it that Crash had plenty to drink, was at her most amusing for him, drove away what she called his 'black devils' and they ended up in a riotous party at a night-club on the Nile.

Crash went home still convinced that it was Amanda whom he loved and whom he wanted eventually as well as his father's fortune.

But the next day he extracted a very real pleasure in giving Lucie all the things that she had never had before.

He took a beautiful suite of rooms for her at the Heliopolis Palace Hotel. Lucie found herself installed in new luxurious surroundings, pinching herself, as she told Crash, to see if she was in a dream or really awake. No more Miss Bryant the hard-working little typist, but Miss Bryant the fiancée of Mr Lorrimer. Her private sitting-room, on a level with the garden, looked out at tall green palms, green lawns and beds of exquisite flowers. She had always admired this place. It lived up to its name, and looked like a palace, with its white domes and turrets pointing to the vivid blue sky.

Her sitting-room was filled with roses. A radio-gramophone was installed for her, with all the latest records that Crash could find in Cairo. Magazines and novels, boxes of chocolates, cigarettes poured in daily. She

106

protested violently that he was giving her too much, but it seemed that he could not do enough. And she did not know that it was because his conscience was working. Blind with happiness, with passionate love for him, she thought that all he did was out of love for her.

During the weeks that followed, a new Lucie evolved from the old. The rather shy and retiring girl blossomed into a radiant young woman with more poise. It was Crash's wish that she should dress as befitted his future wife. There was no need for her to be shabby and out-of-date, he said.

'I'm sickeningly rich,' he told her with his attractive grin, 'and the more you spend, the better I like it. Here's a cheque. Now go and order what you want.'

He amused himself by ordering things with her, too. He boasted that he had taste in women's clothes. She was horrified by his extravagance. He gave her a blue fox-cape to wear over the new, lovely evening dresses which she found in a French shop. There were to be no more cotton frocks run up by a local dressmaker, but the 'last word' in linen or silk dresses, straight from Paris, and in chic hats.

Dozens of boxes arrived at Miss Bryant's rooms full of gorgeous silky lingerie, the thinnest of thin silk stockings and—things that Lucie had always wanted—really expensive shoes and gloves. At Crash's request, she went to a beauty-parlour to have a face-massage, to try a new powder, a new shade of lipstick, and, of course, a new mode of hairdressing. Her make-up was clever, delicate, just right. A clever German hairdresser piled those glossy brown curls of hers high on her head.

X

There came the inevitable day when Crash called at the hotel for his fiancée and found her no longer the pretty, but simple little girl to whom he had proposed, but an exceedingly smart alluring young woman.

It was one of those hot afternoons when nobody in Cairo moved until after tea. Crash brought his car to take Lucie down to the Club. He felt almost bewildered when he looked at her, because it was as though through new eyes. Here was a Lucie fresh from beauty-parlour and hairdresser, sleek and sophisticated, in her linen dress; a new shade of tobacco-brown, with a big straw hat, wide-brimmed on the side of her curly head. Her suede gloves and shoes matched, her bag was perfect. Yellow roses were pinned to her shoulder. Under dark, curled lashes, her hazel eyes looked at him shyly and adoringly. But there was a new pride and dignity in the poise of her young head.

She said:

'Do you like it? Will I do?'

Crash stood still, admiring her.

'I certainly do like it. You know you've changed completely in this last fortnight, Lucie.'

She put down gloves and bag and came up to him, holding out her hands with a charming gesture of surrender.

'Of course, I have. I just live for you, Crash. I no longer belong to myself.'

His cheeks reddened. He had never grown used to this homage from Lucie, and never been able to wipe out the unattractive memory of the reason why he was marrying her. For a moment he stood close to her, holding the two little hands. Why was it she always made him feel so cheap, so rotten?

Last night he had taken Amanda out. But it hadn't been one of their successful evenings. They had wrangled a good bit. Perhaps because he was seeing so much of Lucie, he had started to compare Amanda with her. And last night he had found her hard, *too* hard for a girl. At times even coarse. But Lucie was always very sweet and had a gentle quality which any man must like and respect.

This afternoon, he was struck by her new beauty in the physical sense. Her skin was really exquisite; her face as unlined as a child's; her eyes as clear and as honest. Amanda was not much older, but by heaven, he thought, she looked many years Lucie's senior. He was beginning to think that Amanda made up too heavily, drank too many cocktails and stayed up too late. She was haggard. She would be 'finished' by the time she was thirty-five. But Lucie would stay young forever.

He heard Lucie's soft voice:

'What are you thinking about? You look worried, darling.'

He laughed and kissed each of the small hands he was holding.

'Life does worry me a bit, Lucie.'

'That from you?' she laughed back. '*You* have changed as well as I!'

'I almost think I have,' he said.

'And I feel as though I have emerged from a chrysalis.'

'What a very lovely butterfly!'

As always, she thrilled to his flattery.

'You do say the right thing, Crash.'

'Tell me,' he said, abruptly, 'are you happy?'

She drew a deep breath.

'You know that! I'm living in a sort of marvellous dream.'

His blue restless eyes wandered over her head and round the room.

'Is there anything else you want?'

'Heavens no,' she gasped. 'I've got everything. You've spent far too much money on me, Crash.'

'With admirable results. You look enchanting.'

'I can't think why you chose me, all the same.'

He turned from her, walked to one of the tall windows and looked out for a moment at the dazzling sunshine over the Palace gardens. Lighting a cigarette, he smoked without speaking for a while. Then he felt a light touch on his shoulder, and turned to see Lucie looking up at him anxiously.

'Crash, is there anything wrong?'

'Plenty,' he said, 'but not with you.'

'With you—then?'

'Maybe.'

'Darling, can I help?'

'I think,' he said in a queer voice, 'you *are* helping. You're helping me to see rather straighter than I used to, Lucie.'

Lucie was perplexed. She did not know what he meant. But she had felt, many times since her engagement, that all was not well with her Crash. Much as she loved him, she could not *really* get close to him. There was an indefinable something which separated them and which she did not understand. It had worried her more than a bit. This afternoon she felt it more than ever. She said:

'You don't regret our engagement, do you? If you do, you must say so . . .'

'Well—what if I did?' he asked, almost roughly, 'what if I told you I didn't love you and that I wanted to be free again? How would it affect you, Lucie?'

She looked stunned. Her face turned so pale and her eyes looked so stricken that he made haste to reassure her. Catching her quickly into his arms, he said:

'Don't look like that. I don't want to be free, I assure you. I was only teasing.'

Lucie put her arms around him and held him tightly. She hid her eyes against his shoulder. In a choked voice she said:

'You terrified me. Don't tease me that way. I couldn't *bear* it if you didn't love me or want me any more. You're everything to me . . . *everything.*'

He could feel her heart beating wildly against his. That heart which he knew was so entirely in his keeping. Her trust was infinite, like her love for him.

In that moment the truth hit Crash Lorrimer straight in the eyes. He cared more for this child who had been his fiancée for the last three weeks, much more than he had ever cared for Amanda Portlake. In fact, he was very nearly in love with Lucie. Her absolute goodness, combined with a certain allure which could not be denied, had awakened something within himself which he had not known was there. A new capacity for love. For *real* love. What he had felt for Amanda had been a sham. A selfish passion which would never last. He had had an amusing companionship with her. Perhaps Lucie could never be quite so wickedly amusing. But she

112

was always a charming friend and he was not bored by her, which he had once imagined he would be.

He realised suddenly that things had gone too far. He could not and would not marry this girl, then destroy her belief in him. It would be too ghastly. He would be haunted by such a look as he had just seen on her small face. That stunned look, when she had imagined he no longer wanted her. He was 'everything' to her, and by God, he would try to remain so. He would tell Amanda, this very night, that their affair must end, and they must not meet again.

He would marry Lucie, not only because he wanted the money but because he wanted to love her as she loved him. He would marry her because he wanted her to go on being as happy as she was now.

'Lucie,' he said, huskily, 'my little sweet . . .'

There was a new tenderness in his voice which was more than satisfying to Lucie. She raised her face to his, starry-eyed.

'I love you, Crash.'

'I love you,' he said.

And he said it for the first time in all honesty and for the first time, felt that he could hold up his head amongst men. He was not going to betray either his father's trust or Lucie's.

The kiss they exchanged was long and ardent. When it ended, Lucie looked up at

Crash and saw that his brown, handsome face was radiant. She had never seen him look like that before. It thrilled her to the core. And suddenly he swept off her hat and with his lips against her ear, whispered:

'Can I spoil those lovely curls? Don't let's go down to the Club. Let's stay here alone— just you and I, darling.'

It seemed to her in that moment that she touched the highest pitch of ecstasy. And while she clung to him, she thought that now she understood the meaning of those words:

'Life is made up of moments and it is for these moments that we give our lives.'

That next day at lunch-time, Crash received a peremptory telephone call from Amanda.

'I've had your note,' she said . . . her voice was shaking with anger . . . 'but you can't walk out on me quite as easily as all that, my dear Crash. I'll meet you at the Continental in an hour's time.'

He began to remonstrate. He had said in his note to her that 'for every reason and for all our sakes,' he thought it best they should not meet again. But she was not having it. He would either meet her, she said, or she would present herself at the Mess.

That scared him as she knew it would do. Crash couldn't risk a 'scene' in front of his brother-officers. But he went down to his meeting with Amanda, heavy-hearted. It was not that he bore Amanda any particular ill-will. They had had good times together and he was going to tell her so, and thank her for them. He felt a bit of a cad for breaking with her like this. But surely he was justified! The other thing he had meant to do was so *very* much more caddish.

Any kindly feelings that he retained toward Amanda were speedily choked to death, however, almost at the beginning of his talk with her.

She sat with him in a corner of the lounge which was deserted, and insulted Lucie and himself with a venom which disgusted him. He found himself looking at her coldly, dispassionately, seeing her for the first time as she really was. Bitter, selfish, without principle. Beautiful—yes. But that white and gold beauty no longer held attraction for him. It was just a mask, and what he found under it was ugly and distorted.

'You swore that if you went through with this marriage, you'd get rid of Lucie, then come to me,' she said between clenched teeth. 'You swore it.'

'I know, but I was insane,' he said, quietly, 'I think the shock of seeing what was in my father's Will, and my reluctance to give you up, knocked me right off my rocker.'

'Oh, no, it's now you're off your rocker. You're trying to imagine yourself in love with this miserable . . .'

'Will you stop calling Lucie names or I shall

get up and walk out,' he broke in furiously.

'This is all very different, isn't it? You were ready to call her names, yourself, at one time.'

His face crimsoned.

'I admit that, but I regret it. Isn't that enough for you?'

'No,' she said, and continued her onslaught, her reminders of all that he had ever said or done.

Weary, sick at heart, almost as disgusted with himself as he was with her, Crash tried to end the interview.

'I tell you, Amanda, I can't do what I said. I'm going to marry Lucie and stick to her.'

'Seeing yourself as a family man, dear,' she sneered, 'Lucie the little wife with all the bonny babies and Mr Lorrimer changing his name from "Crash" to "Daddy"?'

He sprang to his feet. Those very blue eyes of his were frozen as they looked down at her.

'You'd better think those things but don't say them to me. Nothing's sacred to you, *nothing.*'

Amanda, too, rose to her feet. She was shaking with fury and disappointment. She saw not only the most attractive of her admirers, but the richest of them, fading from her grasp.

'Nothing was sacred to *you* a short time ago.'

'For which I despise myself.'

'So Lucie is teaching you to walk the straight and narrow path, is she? Shall I send you a Salvation Army uniform for a wedding present?'

He opened his lips to make a hot retort, then controlled himself. In a low voice he said:

'Look here, Amanda, I don't like to part with you on this note. I know I've gone back on what I said—and on what I was—but do try to understand. It's not because I'm becoming pious or anything near it. I merely want to do the right thing by Lucie, and incidentally by my father.'

Silence a moment. Amanda's face was livid under the rouge. Then she said:

'So you're going to marry Lucie Bryant and live happily ever afterwards, eh?'

'I hope so.'

'And does she know *why* you proposed to her in the first place?'

He swallowed hard.

'No, and I hope she never will.'

'I see,' said Amanda. She cocked an eyebrow, pulled a cigarette from an enamel-case, lit it, then turned her back on Crash.

Uneasily he looked after her.

'Aren't you going to say good-bye?'

She turned and glanced at him over her shoulder. The expression in her eyes made him still more uneasy.

'No,' she said, 'because you and I haven't finished with each other yet.'

'Amanda—' he began.

She did not answer and did not turn back

again. After she had gone, he sat down and smoked alone, trying to recover from the nervous tension of that unpleasant interview. What did she mean . . . 'they hadn't finished yet'. They *had!* He would see that they had. He felt a sudden loathing for Amanda. He must, indeed, have been insane to contemplate breaking with Lucie and returning to Amanda. Now, because he had lately been in contact with Lucie he felt there was something almost evil in Amanda. He was thankful to be quit of her. He wanted to wipe her out of his life . . . and with her, all the heavy drinking, the 'beating it up', the waste of his youth and of his gifts. God alone knew he did not wish to become a prig. But he did hope to live decently with Lucie, and *for* Lucie.

Amanda's jeering echoed in his ears. He realised that she would not believe that he should wish to lead a family life and have children. But he did. He would adore to have a child—with Lucie's lovely, honest eyes, and that brave, sweet nature of hers.

He thought of the hour that they had spent together yesterday, in her sitting-room. How adorable she had been to him . . . what a new contentment she had brought him. He felt a sudden aching need for her. A need to forget Amanda, and to forget *himself.*

He pitched his cigarette end away and went out into the sunshine to his car.

In her darkened bedroom, Amanda

118

Portlake lay on her bed with the telephone in one hand and a handkerchief in the other. She had been crying . . . crying not with grief, but with a fury of wounded vanity. Just now she was talking to one of her oldest friends, the wife of a Brigadier-General, who was also a friend of Crash Lorrimer's.

'So there's a felucca-party on tonight, is there?' said Amanda. Her voice was quite controlled and the woman at the other end had no notion of the fires of jealousy and bitterness which were consuming her. 'And you say Crash Lorrimer and his fiancée are in it?'

'Yes, my dear. Of course, if you would rather not come . . . I know you used to be great friends with Crash . . .'

'Oh, not at all,' broke in Amanda, 'I'm very anxious to meet Miss Bryant. I haven't done so yet.'

'Then we shall expect you—nine o'clock. There's a full moon and it ought to be great fun.'

'Thanks awfully,' said Amanda.

She put down the receiver and lay with her hands laced behind her head, thinking. Yes, felucca-parties on a moonlit night could be 'great fun'. She had been on plenty of them last summer with Crash. Crash who rarely emerged from one of them sober. It would be the same old thing. A gay crowd drifting down the Nile on a native boat, with native music to stir the senses. Plenty to eat and drink. Soft cushions in dark corners and oh! yes, Crash could be marvellous on those occasions. But tonight he would be with Lucie. It would be Lucie whom he would hold in his arms, as they floated down the moonlit glamorous river. Lucie whom he was going to marry, and with whom he had suddenly fallen in love.

Amanda clenched her hands until her long nails pierced the palm. She thought:

'I shall be on that felucca, too. And I think it's high time that someone told Miss Lucie Bryant just how much Crash Lorrimer's kisses are worth, and just *why* he is marrying her. Well—that someone, undoubtedly, will be me!'

XI

Tom . . . Tom-tom . . . Tom . . . tom-tom.

The felucca moved slowly down-stream in accompaniment to the throbbing of the native drums. In the bows three Arab musicians played their weird, monotonous music. The soft sobbing sound of it drifted through the warm air which had a velvet quality. It was one of the most beautiful nights that Lucie had known since she came to Egypt. A perfect night with a full moon hanging like a gorgeous honey-coloured disc in the violet-blue sky. A night without wind and with all the languor, the mystery that is forever Egypt.

She sat beside Crash, who had one arm about her shoulders and with his other hand, held fast to her hand. Slowly they had passed under the bridges, away from the city of Cairo, and now there was only desert on either side of them. A fringe of palm-trees that were like black silhouettes carved by the moonlight; an occasional oasis, a clump of mud-huts occupied by the lonely dwellers in the desert; and so bright was the moonlight they could see an infinite distance to a space where desert and sky merged into one vast purple shadow.

Lucie felt like a person in an intoxicating dream. Intoxicated was the word, tonight, she thought. She had never felt her blood run more warmly and ardently through her whole body. She had been on other felucca-parties. They were a favourite pastime on warm nights in Egypt, especially with the Army. But those other parties had meant just an idle flirtation with some young subaltern, or an effort to get away from a less attractive and more elderly admirer. A lot of fun and noise and drink.

But this was different. The fun, the noise, the drink were here just the same. All over the felucca there were couples, many in high spirits, some dancing. Now and then the beauty of the night was spoiled by a shrill burst of laughter or an over-excited voice. But Lucie was deaf, dumb and blind to everything but the charm of the night—and her lover. She felt removed from all these people. Her dream-world was complete—with Crash.

Now and again she looked down at the strong sensitive fingers entwined with hers and thought how she adored Crash and how lucky she was to belong to him . . . to know that in a few weeks' time she would be his wife.

She could not even be upset because Amanda Portlake was on board, although Crash seemed furious. They had come face to face with Amanda soon after the felucca-party had set out. Lucie had been a little surprised because Crash had hardly acknowledged his former girl-friend and his face had grown quite white. At first, Lucie had felt anxious; wondered if that look had come over his face because Amanda still attracted him. Yet if that was the case, why had he proposed to *her?*

As soon as they were alone, she had asked him outright.

'Does Amanda still charm you, darling?'

She had been almost astonished by the vehemence of his reply:

'Not in the slightest. No woman charms me, except you.'

He had put her heart completely at rest. For indeed, it seemed these days that Crash was completely hers. He had changed out of all recognition. His gaiety, his charm remained, but he was indubitably altered; quieter, less reckless and feckless. She could almost describe it as 'settled down'. She thought how delighted old Mr Lorrimer would have been to see him now. The poor dear had worried so unnecessarily about his son. But she, Lucie, had always known that there was nothing to worry about. She had always had faith in Crash, believed that he would come out on top, one day. And her belief was justified.

But it remained to Lucie a complete miracle that *she* should have brought about this transformation. Yet she had; she could not doubt that he loved her. Tonight she was sure of it. He was being so marvellous to her. Wrapped up in her, unaware of the other girls in the party, satisfied to dream here in the shadows, alone with her.

She leaned her head back on the cushion and sighed. Crash Lorrimer heard that sigh and turned his eyes questioningly to the girl beside him.

'Is anything troubling you, my sweet?'

'Why should it be?'

'That sigh . . .'

'Oh, that was just out of pure happiness.'

'You are a darling,' he said, and lifted her hand to his lips.

There was no question now with Crash Lorrimer of marrying Lucie because he wanted his father's money. These past few days he had been telling himself that he would marry her whatever the conditions; even if he were not to gain a penny in the world by his marriage. A miracle had been wrought in him for which he was both humble and grateful. He had fallen in love with the girl of his father's choice. He found her enchanting—adorable—and the fact that she adored him satisfied all his needs. He had never known anything sweeter than Lucie and her love.

She looked especially enchanting tonight, as he had told her when they first met on the felucca. The women were not in evening-dress. Lucie wore a grey-flannel suit and a white organdie blouse with a little stiff bow at the neck. She looked, he had told her, an absolute child, yet such a very soignée young woman these days. Cheeks, eyes, chestnut curls all glowed; and glowed for love of him. He knew it and gloried in the fact.

'I've always been rather bored on these parties,' he told her dreamily. 'Tonight it seems the ideal occupation.'

'That,' said Lucie, 'was what I was thinking.'

'It's a pity we can't float down the river forever—just like this . . .'

He bent his handsome head and touched the warm curve just inside her arm. She shivered a little at the contact of his lips. Sometimes she was almost terrified because of the sensation Crash roused in her. She whispered:

'Darling . . . I love you so much.'

'I'm terribly in love with you,' he said, with conviction, with a new, stirring pride because he spoke the truth.

A man and a woman, arm-in-arm, sauntered

past them. The man was a Major in Crash's own regiment. The woman, in white, with a red fox slung carelessly over one shoulder, was Amanda Portlake.

Crash's hand fell away from Lucie's. She could feel him stiffen, almost freeze, as Amanda passed, glancing in their direction. She could not quite understand why he should feel like that. Somehow, she wished Amanda had not come on this party. But she said nothing. She must be tactful. After all, it was well-known in Cairo that Crash and Amanda used to go round together.

Crash was wishing a good deal more ardently than Lucie that Amanda was not on the felucca. She was the last girl in Egypt whom he wanted to see. Neither did he wish her to come in contact with Lucie. But that, he could not avoid.

During the supper-party they were all together, about a dozen of them, sitting at the tables which had been arranged on deck. Amanda managed to manoeuvre a place exactly opposite Crash and his fiancée. She appeared to be in the highest of spirits, and talked loudly and gaily to them both.

'Fancy seeing old Crash all bound on matrimony. Who would have believed it?' she said with a peal of laughter. 'It just isn't Crash, is it, Eddy?' she turned to the soldier beside her.

Major Edward Crammer, who had never

held much brief for young Lorrimer, mainly because he had more money and better polo-ponies, echoed the laugh.

'Not a bit. Too frightfully un-Crash, what? Been bewitched, eh? Miss Bryant, you're the witch, ha-ha!'

Lucie also joined in the laugh. The Major was a silly, but harmless man. But Crash did not even smile. He was looking with blue, surly eyes at Amanda, remembering how spiteful and unattractive she had been at their last interview.

'This is the first time I've had the pleasure of meeting the future Mrs Crash,' said Amanda. She looked through her long eye-lashes at Lucie. Nobody in that party could guess the fires of jealousy that were eating her up. How she loathed Lucie! Smug-faced little wretch, little prig, oh! she could think of worse names for Lucie Bryant. And Crash was a fool, *a fool.* When he came out of this coma of respectability, of righteousness, he would be bored to death.

'I've often seen you in the Club,' said Lucie, for something to say.

'I don't remember seeing you,' said Amanda with acid sweetness. Then she turned to Crash and said: 'Do you remember the last felucca-party, Crash? You got terribly tight and rolled empty beer-bottles down the deck, and then threw one which landed on the old Arab's drum and went straight through it.'

The party roared with laughter. Crash sat unsmiling. Lucie felt uncomfortable. She knew what Crash was thinking. He was not relishing the memory of those wild days. But Amanda continued with her reminiscences.

'You would have been amused, Lucie. I may call you Lucie, mayn't I?'

She was at her most fascinating throughout the entire supper-party. Charming to Lucie. Charming to Crash, and, finally, so amusing that even Crash, who had no love for her left, had to laugh at some of her jokes. She had always been a witty little devil, he thought. Half the time she was poking fun at him and Lucie, and he knew it, and writhed.

But Lucie was enchanted. She said:

'I do think Amanda is *most* attractive. How on earth you left her side . . .'

'Shut up, darling,' said Crash, softly, yet violently and pressed her hand so tightly that she winced.

It made her smile for sheer happiness. It was so highly flattering to know that Crash *had* deserted this enchanting creature for *her.*

Meanwhile, Amanda played her own game in her own subtle way. She had been especially nice to Lucie and she had won Lucie's sympathy. When the supper-party ended, she took care to drift to Crash's side and say a few words to him. He was forced to reply as politely as possible. Lucie, thinking that she would be tactful, moved a little apart from

127

them. Immediately Amanda said in a voice that she knew would be audible to Lucie:

'It's so marvellous to see you again, Crash. I miss all our good times, horribly.'

Crash scowled. He did not trust Amanda. After what she had said to him at their last meeting, he did not know what game she was playing. She added:

'There's so much to look forward to . . . but perhaps I'd better not talk about that . . .'

Crash went hot, then cold. What *was* the woman driving at? Lucie, lighting a cigarette, was thoughtful. She, too, wondered what Amanda meant by those words. What *had* she to look forward to? To what did she refer?

Amanda went straight from Crash to Lucie's side; tucked an arm through hers and moved with her along the deck.

'Come along, let's powder our noses.'

Crash gazed dubiously after the two girls. He could not bear to see them together. He sensed something evil behind Amanda. Yet he did not know what it was. With a passionate love of Lucie he looked after her small figure. She was much shorter than Amanda. A darling child in that grey flannel suit, with her brown curls. He could find nothing to excite him even one fraction in Amanda's tall slenderness and sophisticated platinum head. Indeed, when he looked at the red fox swinging over her shoulder, he thought:

'She's rather like a vixen, herself . . .'

128

Below deck, Amanda suddenly became serious with Lucie. She assumed an expression of bitter sadness.

'You don't know what it means to me,' she said under her breath, 'to see you with Crash.'

Lucie felt hot and uncomfortable.

'I'm so terribly sorry . . .'

'I think you'd be still more sorry if you knew the truth.'

Lucie's golden eyes looked puzzled.

'The truth about what?'

'Crash . . . his proposal to you . . . the whole thing.'

Lucie paused in the act of taking a powder-puff from her bag. She felt a sudden chill as though an icy wind had shivered through the glamorous night and touched her.

'I honestly don't know what you're driving at.'

Amanda bit her lip. Then suddenly she seized Lucie's hand.

'You ought to know. It's only fair. You *ought* to know what he's done to you. You're such a dear little thing. I don't think you should be deceived like this. I honestly don't!'

Lucie shook her head, bewildered. A queer distaste made her withdraw her hand from Amanda's long pointed fingers.

'Please!' she protested.

But Amanda went on in a rush:

'You ought not to marry Crash without realising why he proposed to you. You don't know the terms of old Lorrimer's Will, do you? But I do. He left his money to Crash on condition that he married you. And Crash was in love with me. Crash promised to marry me. But he had to break with me because of that Will . . .' she gave an hysterical little laugh . . . 'break with me temporarily, anyhow. He wanted the money. He wanted me, too, but he said he must marry you first, and then come back to me. It sounds disgraceful, despicable. But I love him as much as you do. And I suppose I'd stoop to anything to get him.'

Lucie stood still. She was as ice-cold now as though the temperature of the night had fallen below zero. A nervous trembling seized her. Her breath came quickly and unevenly. For a moment she could neither speak nor move. It took her several seconds to take in what Amanda was telling her. Amanda was now embroidering on the situation. Lucie listened. She had to listen. But it was almost too much for her. Amanda's voice was accompanied by a roaring in her ears as though somebody had hit her violently over the head. And it was a mortal blow. It was killing her, mentally, as sure as she stood there.

She could not doubt what Amanda was saying. She had only to go to the Registrar and she could see the Will. (It had never entered Lucie's head to do so.) So *that* was the explanation of Crash's sudden proposal. *That* was why he had changed so suddenly from the boy who used to take little or no notice of her, into an eager suitor for her hand? It had been old Lorrimer's wish that he should marry her, and he had made it a stipulation in his Will. Crash could not inherit the money unless he carried out those terms. In other words *he was marrying her for the money.* Suddenly the realisation of it all smote Lucie fully. It forced a moan from her lips:

'Oh God, my *God.*'

'Poor Lucie,' said Amanda, 'pretty tough on you, isn't it? And I feel ashamed now that I ever had a hand in the bargain. Only Crash wouldn't be satisfied until I'd sworn to stick to him, even after he was married to you.'

Lucie made a terrific effort to pull herself together, but her teeth were chattering as though she had ague. Amanda's last words had hoisted down the flag of her pride, and it lay torn in tatters at her feet. She had loved Crash so much. It had been almost an idolatrous love. Perhaps she had loved him too much and this was her punishment. She could no longer hold up her head and feel that the most attractive man in Cairo had asked her to marry him because he loved her. He was marrying her because of the money and he was going to keep Amanda behind her back. The humiliation was bitter beyond enduring. And it was so horrible to think that Crash could be guilty of such rottenness.

Amanda spoke again.

131

'You mustn't tell him. Oh, Lucie, you mustn't tell him or else he'll kill me. Have pity on me. Be sorry for us both. We love each other, you see.'

Then Lucie found her voice.

'Do you? I should have thought if you two had loved, you would have married on nothing. I'd have been glad to marry Crash if he hadn't had a penny in the world.'

Amanda had the grace to change colour. She said:

'Perhaps we're not like that. Crash wouldn't be happy on nothing. You ought to know that.'

Lucie did know it. She could see quite plainly that Crash just wouldn't be 'Crash' if he was penniless; out of the regiment; without his polo-ponies, without all that ready cash which he liked to fling about so extravagantly. (Oh, God, how she hated the thought, now, of all that he had given her, and *why*.)

'If you love him, Lucie, don't let him down,' said Amanda.

Lucie felt as though she was being tortured.

'Let him down? Good God, what has he done to me?'

'He was forced into it by that Will.'

'It was monstrous,' said Lucie in a strangled voice, 'and Mr Lorrimer, whom I thought my friend, did me the worst turn of his life when he made that Will.'

'But you won't refuse to marry Crash so that he loses the money?'

For a moment Lucie made no reply. It was on the tip of her tongue to say: *'Why not? Why should I care what he loses? Why shouldn't he be made a pauper, and why shouldn't I laugh at him after the irreparable harm he has done me?'*

But the words did not come. Her mind moved in other directions. So great was her love for this man that it could not die in an hour, a night. Indeed, it could never die. She knew that as surely as she stood here, facing the girl who had opened her eyes to the horrible truth. She alternated between loathing Amanda and being grateful to her. Yes, she could be grateful because it would have been ghastly to go on living in her fool's paradise; to marry Crash and think herself an adored wife, only to have him leave her eventually for Amanda. It was best that she should know where she was.

Her first reaction was to tell him what she knew, and run away. Tell him that she could not see him again. Yet if she did that she would reduce him to penury. That would be awful for Crash. He might go down . . . and down. And she would always have it on her conscience that it was through *her.*

Little matter to her now that she knew why Crash wanted to marry her. It was the end for her. The end of her dreams, of her wild sweet romance. And since it was the end of all things, why not go through with the marriage and let Crash have what he wanted. The money *and* Amanda.

Her face looked so pinched, so grey, that even Amanda was anxious.

'Can I get you a drop of brandy,' she asked.

'No, thank you.'

'You aren't going to tell Crash, are you?'

'No, I don't think I am. I don't think I care what happens to me now. Let him have what he wants. It's all the same to me.'

Amanda felt a cringe of real compunction. Bad though she was, she felt ashamed in the presence of this real love—a love which was prepared to make any sacrifice. Only dimly could she guess what Lucie was suffering. She said:

'I'm really very sorry, Lucie, but Crash *was* mine before his father died and . . .'

'I quite understand,' broke in Lucie, 'please don't say any more.'

'Then you're really going through with it?'

'Yes. I don't want Crash or anybody else to lose a fortune through me,' said Lucie, bitterly.

'Oh, I think you're grand,' began Amanda. But Lucie cut her short and turned and walked blindly out of sight.

Amanda shrugged her shoulders, and applied a powder-puff to her rather flushed face.

What a strange girl! She really was rather sporting. A bit stupid, too. It was a bit stupid for any woman to give as much as Lucie was

prepared to give Crash, but it suited Amanda
...*so what?*

Lucie did not rejoin Crash immediately. She
fled out of sight to a dark corner in the felucca,
put her arms on the rails and leaned her face
upon them. She felt physically ill. Stricken as
though by a blight which was going to creep
gradually all through her and destroy her.
After her adoration, her pride in Crash's love,
to know the real reason why he was marrying
her seemed terrible to bear. Yet she must bear
it. She had no alternative. Either she must go
through with the marriage and give him what
he wanted, or disappear and leave him with
nothing. She might argue with herself that the
latter course was what he deserved, but that
did not matter. Her nature was not a malicious
one. In spite of the mortal wrong which she
thought Crash had done her, she had no wish
to pay him back. She could even pity him. Poor
Crash! He wasn't all that bad. At times his
conscience must have smote him badly. Yes,
she could pity him.

'But, dear God,' she whispered, through dry
lips, 'I pity myself tonight. *I pity myself!*'

For some time she stayed there alone in the
starlight, while the felucca turned its course,
drifted back toward Cairo, and wrestled with
herself. And gradually there came across her
the conviction that she could only prove her
real love for Crash if she carried this wedding
through, let him get away with the money—

and Amanda.

She could not tell him that she knew. That would make the position quite insupportable. She could not face him with the truth. It would only result in an encounter which would humiliate them both and make it impossible for them to carry on. She would marry him. But she would never really live with Crash. Her whole body grew hot at that thought. Then she began to feel sorry for Crash for another reason. It must have been difficult for him to act the lover all this time. Well, he should never be made to act the *husband*. She would leave him directly after their wedding and then he could go to Amanda and put an end to the farce.

This night on the felucca had started so gloriously. She had never been more in love or felt a greater rapture. And this was the end— this disillusionment and despair.

Crash found her. He had been searching the felucca, anxiously. He came straight up to her and seized her in his arms.

'Lucie, my sweet, where have you been? Why are you standing here all alone?'

For a moment she made no answer. Her small body was rigid in his embrace. She told herself that of course he felt guilty . . . worried as to what Amanda had been saying to her. That was his trouble . . . conscience. He was not in the least anxious about *her* happiness . . . only his own.

136

'Lucie,' Crash repeated her name, 'are you all right, darling? What's happened?'

Then she made the biggest effort of her life. She knew that if she was to carry through this wedding for his sake, she must do it properly. She put her arms around his neck and hid her face against his heart. A grey, pinched little face with stricken eyes. But he could not see it. She said in a muffled voice:

'You'll never never know how much I love you, Crash.'

With a sigh of relief, he hugged her close to him. He was so afraid that Amanda had been vindictive and done too much talking. But such was obviously not the case. He said:

'I love you in the same way, my little sweet.'

She did not move, did not answer what she believed to be a shameful lie. She kept her desperate young face pressed against his heart. But she wished that she could die like this, die before this agony in her mind became unendurable.

XII

Lucie was a character who never did things by halves. When she loved, she loved completely. Even to the annihilation of herself. And that was how she cared for Crash Lorrimer. So, in those few weeks before her wedding, she was able to subject herself completely, and prove her love to Crash to the uttermost.

Not by word or by deed did she allow Crash to know what Amanda had told her. A few days before her marriage, she telephoned to Amanda.

'I want you to realise,' she said, 'that I shall leave Crash immediately the ceremony is over and he can claim his money, I shall disappear. You can have him and you need not fear that I shall turn up again.'

She put up the receiver before Amanda could answer her. She felt that she could not bear any form of discussion with the other girl.

The bitterness of those days left a mark on her. She lost some of that bloom, that glow which Crash liked to see on her face. At times she looked so pale and there was such a hunted look in her eyes, that he was worried— uneasy. But when he questioned her, Lucie assured him that it was her health. Just 'nerves'. He believed her and took it for granted that she needed a change of air. It didn't do for a woman to be too long in Cairo, especially during the hot weather. He made marvellous plans for their honeymoon. She listened to them stoically, knowing that she would never experience all that might have been hers in other circumstances. But it hurt . . . oh God, how wildly it hurt to hear Crash talking about his two months' leave . . . half of which he wished her to spend in the South of

France and the other half in England.

At times she was staggered by his powers of acting. She could have sworn that he seemed happy and excited about it all. Yet he was acting . . . it was all for the sake of the money. She knew it now. And while she listened to him and agreed to everything, and suffered him to hold her and kiss her, she felt as though she was dying inwardly. A slow, suffocating death.

How to get through her wedding-day was a problem which made even her brave young heart quail. On the night before, which she spent with the wife of Crash's Colonel who had kindly consented to see her through . . . (the Colonel was giving her away) . . . Lucie had an hour or two of blind panic which made her long to disappear now, tonight, before she could meet Crash and take her vows to him. It seemed wicked, purposeless to do so. Yet no, it was all to one purpose. A vile, mercenary one. Crash must have his money *and* his Amanda. If she turned coward and ran away now, he would lose that money and anything might happen to him. She tried so hard not to care. Tried to feel for him the contempt he deserved. But she could only go on loving him. That was her secret torment. Her idol had crashed, but the broken pieces were still there in her heart.

Because of the recent death of Mr Lorrimer, it had been decided that they should not have a showy wedding. They would be married quietly before the Registrar, and afterwards go straight to Heliopolis, take a Misr 'plane to Alexandria and go thence by boat to Venice where their honeymoon was to begin.

An unspeakable bitterness was Lucie's when she finally went to that wedding with Crash Lorrimer. A bitterness accentuated by the fact that everything on the surface seemed so marvellous. The day . . . hot, cloudless, a miracle of gold and blue. Egypt at its best. Herself, the bride, in a white suit, with Crash's blue foxes over one arm, and a white hat with a rakish pink veil tied in a big bow in Edwardian fashion behind her brown head. Pearls round her neck, and diamond clips—Crash's wedding present; all the officers in the regiment turning out to see their polo-playing favourite married to the girl of his choice.

What a day it should have been! What a marvellous day it *might* have been.

Crash was in hilarious spirits. He was all unconscious of Lucie's self-torture. The Crash of old days, gay, heart-breakingly handsome, white flower in his button-hole, the most debonair figure in Cairo. And a look on his face when Lucie joined him, which made her sick with shame. How *could* he fake such a look . . . such an expression of intense love and humility! It was monstrous, when all the time he meant to go behind her back the moment they returned from the honeymoon, and carry on his *liaison* with Amanda.

But Crash knew nothing of what was passing in Lucie's mind. He looked into those golden eyes of hers which were a bit of a mystery to him these days, and said:

'This is the happiest day of my life, darling.'

But she thought:

'And the most tragic of mine . . .'

Then the wedding was over, and they were driving to Gezira to the flat where the Colonel's wife was holding a reception for them.

Lucie Bryant was now Mrs Conrad Lorrimer, with her marriage certificate in her bag and a new platinum ring on her finger. Crash insisted upon driving her alone in their Bentley to Gezira. He told her how lovely she was and how gloriously proud he was of his newly-made wife.

She listened to him almost amazed. He was such an incredible actor. Or perhaps he was physically in love with her just for the moment. A man could be like that . . . capable of faked emotions when his senses were stirred. Perhaps he might be amused to remain married to her, *and* keep Amanda in the background. Lucie almost hated him for that. Hated him on this, her wedding-day, which should have been the greatest day of her life.

But she, too, had her plans, and they were nothing to do with Crash's; there was to be no

141

Misr 'plane or Venice for her. While the wedding-guests were drinking champagne, Crash in their midst, Lucie slipped away and changed from her white clothes into an old grey-flannel suit. Under the bed, unknown to the Colonel's wife, she had a small bag packed. And downstairs there was a hired car with a chauffeur waiting for her. She had saved for this moment . . . saved some of the money which Crash had given her for her trousseau. And on that she must live until she found a suitable job.

While Crash was still responding to the toasts of his friends, the Colonel's wife searched her flat in a bewildered way for the missing bride. But Lucie Lorrimer sat in her hired car driving grimly out of Cairo, and on to the Alexandria road.

The sight of the desert was blurred by the great tears that came into her eyes and rolled slowly down her face. Blindly she took off her wedding ring, dropped it into her bag and whispered:

'I've done it. You've got what you want, Crash, and you won't have to be worried with *me* any more. It's good-bye. Good-bye to you and to love, and—good-bye to poor Mrs Conrad Lorrimer!'

XIII

Crash Lorrimer put down his champagne glass and suddenly realised that his bride had been missing from the room for quite a long time.

He threaded his way through the crowd of wedding guests. It was a baking hot day and despite all electric fans, the room was close and full of smoke. He pulled at his collar and shook his head.

'Phew! I shall be glad to get out of this,' he thought, 'but where's my little Lucie?'

He met the Colonel's wife at the door. With his schoolboy grin, he hailed her:

'Ah, Mrs Langham, what's happened to my wife?'

Olive Langham was a woman who always kept her head in a moment of crisis. She did not lose it now. But under its customary make-up, her patrician face was definitely pale. She took the young bridegroom by the arm and led him out of the room.

'Come where it's quiet, Crash, I want to speak to you.'

The laughter sped from Crash's blue eyes. He walked with Mrs Langham into the hall.

'What's wrong? Where's Lucie?'

'That,' said Olive Langham, 'is the question. Where *is* Lucie?'

It took only five minutes for Crash's quick

mind to grasp the situation. Lucie had disappeared. Disappeared as completely as though the earth had swallowed her up. For the last twenty minutes, Olive Langham and her *suffragis* had been searching the flat. A few moments ago, one of them had gone downstairs to speak to the Sudanese porter in charge of the building. The porter had informed him that a lady carrying a suitcase had come down from Mrs Langham's flat, stepped into a big car and driven away. But where to, he could not tell.

From his description, it was obvious that it was Lucie who had gone away in that car.

Once he realised it, Crash's brain registered further conclusions. If Lucie had run away, there was only one person in Cairo responsible. Amanda! Amanda had said something. Lucie *knew.*

Crash did not wait to make any explanations to the baffled wife of his Colonel. He turned from her and walked straight back into the crowded reception-room to look for Amanda. Amanda whom he had *had* to ask to his wedding because of her father.

Crash's face was no longer flushed and happy. It was almost grey. And in his eyes was a look of fear. The dark fear that somebody . . . something . . . had removed Lucie from him forever.

He walked straight up to Amanda. She happened to be alone at that moment, standing in front of a mirror, adding a touch to her already heavily blackened lashes. She was looking particularly attractive and pleased with herself.

'Oh, hel-*lo*, Crash,' she greeted him sweetly. She had watched him come up behind her, in the mirror.

Without ceremony, roughly, he seized her arm.

'What have you said to Lucie?'

'My dear Crash . . .'

'Cut out that stuff. What have you said to Lucie? She's gone. She's run away. Why, good God, we've only been married an hour. Something's happened and nobody in the world but you can be responsible.'

Amanda swallowed. Her face changed from red to white and from white to red again. But she flung back that fair, curled head of hers and looked defiantly, brazenly at the man who had once been her lover.

'You didn't want to keep Lucie with you, did you? Your original plan was to marry her, get the money and then come back to me. Well . . . now you can do it. So why worry?'

For a moment Crash stood still. His face was livid and his eyes black with fury. If he could have killed Amanda in that moment, he would have done so.

For he knew, not only what she had done to him, but to Lucie. He said:

'If you don't want me to murder you here,

where you stand, Amanda, you had better tell me the truth. What did you say to Lucie, and when?'

She shrugged her shoulders.

'You really are rather boring these days, Crash. You take everything so seriously. I just told Lucie on the felucca that night that she ought to know why you were marrying her. And, after all, I think it was only fair that she *should* know the truth. So I told her.'

Another silence. Crash breathed hard and fast. Then he said under his breath:

'You *devil*.'

'My dear Crash, if you're so virtuous these days, surely you advocate the truth. Why should poor Lucie be deceived?'

It was with the greatest difficulty that the man controlled himself. He was shaking from head to foot. Sheer primitive rage made him long to put his hands round Amanda's long white throat, and strangle the life out of her. She had told Lucie the truth. His poor little Lucie! Poor tender-hearted child! Now he understood why she had looked so ill at times since that felucca party; why she had in some inexplicable way changed. She knew why in the first instance he had wanted to marry her. But, of course, she did not know that now he loved her as much as she loved him, and that he would have married her even if it had meant losing the money.

Amanda said:

'Do let go of my arm, you're hurting me.'

'I wish I could hurt you as you deserve to be hurt,' he said. But his hands fell away from her, loathing her. He added: 'And would you mind telling me exactly what impression you left upon Lucie? Did you let her think that I still wanted to do her down and go off to you, once we were married?'

'I told her the truth,' said Amanda stubbornly, 'I told her exactly what you promised. You haven't done her down. You've done me down. That's how it really is.'

'Oh, no it isn't. I told you weeks ago that I regretted that arrangement, bitterly. Oh God . . .' Crash broke off and put a clenched hand up to his head. He felt as though he was going crazy. 'What must Lucie think of me, what she must think . . . and how she must be suffering . . .'

'What about my suffering?' demanded Amanda.

'You!' he said, and the contempt in his voice withered her up. 'If you suffer, Amanda, you deserve it. You deserve all that's coming to you in this world and in the next for what you've done. I trusted you when I told you the terms of my father's Will. You knew that I did not wish Lucie to be told. You knew that I wanted to do the decent thing by her and wipe out the past. What you've done is so low that there isn't a word for it. You've shattered that child's belief in me and you've ruined all chances of

147

our happiness. Well . . . if that's what you wanted, I hope you're satisfied.'

He swung round on his heel. Amanda, who was beginning to wonder if she had gained anything by her treachery, felt suddenly afraid. She called after him.

'Crash . . . wait.'

He looked over his shoulder.

'There's only one thing you can do and that is to tell me where Lucie is.'

'I don't know,' said Amanda sullenly.

'Have you any idea at all what she meant to do. Come on . . . out with it. You've done so much harm already, you ought to do any mortal thing you can to undo it.'

'Oh, to the devil with all that,' said Amanda in the same sullen voice. 'And anyhow, I don't know where your precious Lucie is. She said she meant to go through with the wedding so that you could have the cash and then leave you with me. That was her wish.'

'Her wish!' repeated Crash. His voice was wild with a bitterness of pain which he had never dreamed he could feel. He, who had never known a moment's unhappiness. He who had laughed his way through life. The gay, spoiled Crash who had had every woman in Cairo at his feet. The irresponsible Crash whose code had been: *'Eat, drink and be merry, for tomorrow we die.'* He knew differently now. He knew that it didn't pay to go through life quite like that. And he knew that there was

148

only one woman in the world for him, and that was Lucie, his wife. *His wife.* Good God, he could scarcely call her that, and he had lost her already.

He walked blindly out of the room and into the hall. As he did so, he tore the white flower out of his button-hole and flung it on the floor. That flower had been an emblem of festivity. But this was no longer a festive occasion. It was an occasion for mourning. It was the blackest day of his life. A jealous woman had let him down. But much worse than that . . . she had let Lucie down . . . she had hurt Lucie. It was that thought which hit Crash hardest. The idea of what Lucie must have suffered ever since that felucca party. What untold agonies of disillusionment and pain she must have endured, believing him to be the lowest cad on earth. And believing that he had faked his love for her. In the beginning it had been true, but not now. *Not now!* And whatever happened, he must find her and explain. He must *make* her believe that he loved her now and that Amanda had lied.

Mrs Langham waylaid him in the hall.

'Have you found out anything? Crash, you look awful . . .'

'I feel awful,' he cut in, 'but look here, Mrs Langham, for the love of heaven, don't let this become too public, for a bit. I don't want there to be a scandal. Give out that Lucie has been taken suddenly ill and that she's not able to go

149

away to-day. And just get rid of the guests as soon as you can. I'm going to look for Lucie.'

Olive Langham gasped.

'But where is she? Why did she run away?'

'That,' said Crash, 'I'll try to explain to you later.'

The Colonel's wife, bewildered, returned to her drawing-room to spread the news of Lucie's sudden illness, as Crash suggested. But it all seemed very peculiar to her. As far as she could remember, Lucie had been quite all right first thing this morning . . . quite happy . . . and such a *lovely* bride . . . what had possessed the girl to rush away alone, so mysteriously.

The rest of that day for Crash Lorrimer was a nightmare. All through the long, sunny hours that followed his wedding, he raced round Cairo in his car like a demented being, searching for the girl who had only been made his wife that day. But the search was to no avail. Nobody had seen Lucie and her car. And that Lucie was no longer in Cairo, he was now confident. He had been into every hotel, every possible place where she might be hiding. Tonight he was forced to realise that she had left the city. And she might have gone on two roads. To Alexandria or to Port Said. A search might prove futile in either of those places. A girl could soon change her name and disappear in Egypt, if she *wanted* to.

He had tried everything. At every garage in

150

Cairo he made enquiries. But whoever had hired that car out to Lucie had obviously been well bribed. Nobody gave her away. The only thing Crash could do was to discover whether or not she had left Egypt. He got in touch with the authorities at both Alexandria and Port Said, telling them to let him know at once should a Mrs Lorrimer attempt to book a passage on any of the outgoing boats. She had a new passport in his name. She could not get away without producing that passport, so he had her there!

The end of that day found him sitting with Olive Langham in her flat which was now quiet and deserted, talking things over. If ever Olive Langham had been sorry for a man, she was sorry for this young subaltern now. He had always been popular with her, as with most regimental wives in Cairo. She knew that he had been a bit wild. Occasionally the Colonel had called him a 'damned young fool'. But they had always liked Crash.

She had never seen a more dejected picture than he made tonight. He looked ill and haggard. He refused to drink, but sat smoking one cigarette after another, talking of Lucie as though she were already dead.

'It's obvious,' he said, 'she thinks I've married her because of the money and she was much too proud to stay. It's so typical of little Lucie to think of others before herself. She went through with the marriage for my sake.

And how it must have hurt her . . . *oh God, how it must have hurt . . .!'*

It was that sort of cry, and others like it, that went to Mrs Langham's heart. She talked to young Lorrimer as though she were his mother. And she refused to allow him to descend quite so utterly into the depths. She knew the story now—the whole of it. He had thought it best to tell her. She was a woman of discretion and not likely to give him away. He reviled himself for what he meant to do in the first place. But even that, Mrs Langham would not allow.

'You were tempted by that wretched Portlake girl. I've always loathed her. I'm not going to admit that you did right in the first place, Crash, but the real wrong lies at Amanda's door. She had no right to tell Lucie what she did. On your own admission, you have grown to love Lucie and it is that which we must make her understand.'

Crash raised a haggard desperate young face.

'If we ever find her, Mrs Langham.'

'We will. We must,' she said.

But it was easier said than done, and in the weeks that followed, not only Crash's hopes sank to rock bottom, but Olive Langham's with them. Despite all influence, all efforts made by both the military and civil authorities, the girl who had been Mrs Conrad Lorrimer only for a short time, remained lost. Lost as though the

152

desert itself had swallowed her up.

Many a time during that black and unforgettable period of his life, Crash remembered how once before Lucie had been lost. Actually in the desert, itself, and it was there he had really found her. How first she had gained his admiration by her courage, and later his love by the very charm and sweetness of her. And it seemed to him awful that this should be the end of their love. Misunderstanding on her part, and no chance for him to explain and to make up to her what he knew she must have endured since Amanda betrayed him.

The strain of the futile search for Lucie began to tell on Crash, strong and young though he was. And finally he made up his mind that there was only one thing to do. If he did not find her soon, he would resign his commission. He would not take the money his father had left. Not under these conditions. Not unless Lucie was installed in her rightful position as his wife. He would not accept her sacrifice. He would show her *somehow* that he would give his life to wipe out the past and live with her as his father had wished them to live.

But now he began to wonder, and so indeed did Olive Langham, whether Lucie was alive. Whether Crash would ever be given the chance to right the wrong he had done her. Whether, indeed, one of these days her young body would be found in the Nile. Whether, in her unhappy state of mind *she had killed herself.*

That began to be a terror to Crash from which he could not get away. He was on the verge of a nervous breakdown when the Colonel sent him into the Western desert on manoeuvres, knowing that the enforced work combined with the complete peace of those great wastes, might keep him from breaking.

XIV

And while all this was going on in Cairo, Lucie Lorrimer, herself, was very much alive, physically, hidden from the world in a villa eight hundred miles up the Nile, between Cairo and Khartoum.

The solitude and exile that Lucie had wanted after her marriage to Crash had been offered to her within twenty-four hours of her arrival in Alexandria. She had had what she thought an unexpected stroke of luck. She had gone straight to the Cecil Hotel. It was the biggest and most expensive one in Alexandria, and she had no intention of remaining there. But it was the only one she knew, so she had decided to stay there for one night. At dinner, she had found herself at a table beside an Egyptian family, the head of which was Ramdan Pasha, a wealthy cotton-merchant who had at one time had interests in old Lorrimer's petroleum company.

The Pasha, himself, had frequently been received in the offices by Mr Lorrimer's secretary and therefore knew Lucie well.

She liked him. He was one of the nicest types of Egyptian. An enormously fat, grey-haired man with kindly eyes, and a red *tarboosh* sticking at rather a grotesque angle on his huge black head. He was staying at the Cecil Hotel with his wife and daughter. The daughter, aged fourteen, had just returned from a Swiss school. The Pasha now wished her to perfect her English. They were going up the Nile to their summer villa and suggested that Lucie should accompany them. She could teach English to Ferial, the daughter, in return for which she would receive a good salary, added to which Lucie knew she would lead a very luxurious life. The wealth of the Ramdans was colossal.

It was the sort of God-given chance which Lucie snapped up at once. She determined to tell the old Pasha her story and her reason for wishing to remain hidden from everybody who knew her in Cairo. The Egyptian was interested and sympathetic.

'In our place in Upper Egypt, you will be lost to the world,' he told her. 'You need have no fears.'

So, that next morning, Lucie, once more 'Miss Bryant', left Alexandria with Ramdan

Pasha, his wife and daughter, in the capacity of companion and tutor to the girl.

From that hour onward, Lucie felt that her life was unreal. It was as though she became detached from herself. The real Lucie was a completely broken-hearted woman, desperately lonely and alone, and with only one thought ever present in her mind, the memory of Crash whom she had loved so utterly. Crash to whom she belonged by the law, but who was remote from her because of his treachery, his unforgivable conduct toward her. Crash whom she wanted to hate and forget. But she could do neither. She could only go on loving and missing him intolerably and wondering if the sharpness of the pain in her heart would ever grow less. Indeed, at moments she felt that she was dying . . . slowly dying from an incurable malady.

But the other Lucie was a calm, reserved young woman who did her job thoroughly, if automatically and gave every satisfaction to the Ramdan family. She was charming to look at, well-dressed. They liked that. She had a distinction which was essentially English, therefore a good example to their daughter. She could play tennis with Ferial, swim with her, enjoy music with her. At the end of a fortnight, she was indispensable, and Ferial adored her. But only the old Egyptian, himself, understood what was going on behind that composure and the true significance of the tragic hopelessness in those large hazel eyes which Lucie turned upon the world. He was enormously impressed by her courage.

'It is the courage of the English,' he would tell himself. 'They are a brave race. She neither weeps nor wails nor bemoans her fate aloud, as an Egyptian woman would do. If Allah is merciful, he will restore to her this man whom she loves.'

But Allah did not appear to be merciful to Lucie during the weeks that followed. She had deliberately cut herself away from Crash and from any of the people who might try to find her. And she took it for granted that nobody was trying. Crash would obviously be pleased that she had disappeared. She was his wife. Legally, he was now entitled to his father's money, and he could go on having a very good time with Amanda. In due time he could annul their marriage on the grounds that she refused to live with him. That must, surely, be just what he required.

Sometimes she thought how in happier circumstances she might have enjoyed living in the Ramdans' villa. It was a dream-place. No money had been spared. A long, white building with wide verandahs and balconies on the very banks of the Nile. At a great cost, a glorious garden had been made out of a desert. An English garden, full of roses, and herbaceous flowers which at times made Lucie's heart ache for England. The vivid blue of delphinium and lupins, the scarlet and pink of peonies, vivid borders of spice carnations, great tawny lilies, and giant hollyhocks. Gentle English flowers set against an exotic background of spiky palm-trees, the deep green waters of the Nile—and beyond, the desolate African wastes. A queer retreat from the world, and a very lovely one. Lucie was never tired of wandering in that garden.

The house itself was a miracle of comfort and modern luxury. Lucie had a huge bedroom, her own bathroom and a servant especially to wait upon her. Outside, there was a swimming pool, hard tennis courts, and even a skating rink.

At a fantastic cost, the Pasha had brought machinery here for freezing the water, and made a rink so that his spoiled child could skate, even though the temperature in the early summer months rose to over ninety degrees.

All this luxury, sunlight, good food and plenty of exercise, kept Lucie physically well. But she was painfully thin by the end of her first month with the Ramdans. And at moments she felt as though every bit of vitality was being drained from her.

For Ferial's sake, she tried to be companionable. It cost her an effort when her heart was secretly crying out for Crash and for the old life. She knew that she would have given her soul to see him just for a few moments, and to live again in that fool's paradise which Amanda had so rudely shattered. A paradise in which she had believed that Crash loved her; when in his arms she had reached the ultimate of love, of loving.

There were moments when she concentrated on the memory of him and felt that she was breaking . . . that it could not be long before her life ended. *She could not go on without him.* She understood now the meaning of those words which Tennyson had written:

'*Sweet as remembered kisses after death,*
And sweeter far than those by hopeless
  fancy feigned
On lips that are for others . . .
Oh, death in life, the days that are no more!'

That was exactly how she felt, here in the Egyptian's wonderful summer residence. It was *a death in life,* and soon life itself would be extinct.

Pride had no place in this. She could try to be proud, to despise Crash for what he had done, but it was no use. She knew that she would love him until the end of all things.

She had kept the ring which he had put on her finger when they were married, on that day which seemed a thousand years ago. Sometimes when she was alone at night, she would stand on the balcony outside her room and look across the moonlit Nile in the direction of Cairo. She would slip the wedding ring on her finger and concentrate on the memory of Crash and all that he had meant to her. Drearily she would wonder how he was, what he was doing, and if he ever thought of her. Yes, no doubt he did. There was a good side to Crash. She had always said so. That good side would conquer at times, and his conscience would prick him. Perhaps sometimes when Amanda was in his arms, he would remember his *wife*. But what was the good of memories, Lucie asked herself, hopelessly. And she would turn from the beauty and romance of the Egyptian night, fling herself on her luxurious bed and cry until dawn.

For two months she led that life. For two months she devoted herself to Ferial and to the service of her Egyptian employers who were always kind and considerate. But as time wore on, Lucie wondered whether she could get through the whole summer. Not only was the heat beginning to be unbearable, but the whole thing was killing her by inches. She had an intolerable longing to return to Cairo, find Crash and see him again, if only once again . . . And that feeling terrified her. She could not, *would not* be so utterly lacking in pride, she told herself. She had made this sacrifice for him and she must go through with it.

Perhaps one of the hardest things that Lucie

160

had to endure that summer was complete separation from people of her own race. The Pasha, his wife and daughter were English speaking people, but they were not *English.* And up here where the Ramdans' villa had been built, no English tourists ever came.

She was given many opportunities to go down to Luxor where the tombs in the Valley of the Kings drew continual visitors. But at this time of year, the big hotels were shut and in any case, Lucie could not risk being seen there, in case she came in contact with someone from Cairo who knew Crash and herself and could give the whole show away.

The long, difficult days of her self-imposed retreat went on, like a slow death. The first time that she emerged from it was when a private seaplane came down on the Nile only a few hundred yards from the Ramdans' villa and the whole household was flung into the excitement of rescuing its occupants.

There were two English officers in that 'plane, both on leave from Khartoum. The Ramdan household was having the usual afternoon siesta at the moment when the machine struck the water. The first that Lucie heard of it was from the daughter of the house. Ferial, her big brown eyes brilliant with excitement, came rushing into the bedroom where Lucie lay dozing under her mosquito net.

'Mees! . . . Mees! . . . Come at once and see

what has happened.'

Lucie slipped quickly into a cotton frock and some sandals and hurried downstairs with the girl. Once outside the villa, she could see several of the Pasha's native servants rowing frenziedly across the glittering river towards a 'plane which was floating, not apparently badly damaged, but with the engine put out of action so that for the moment the pilot could not 'take off' again. Later, it was explained that owing to a mechanical defect, the engine had seized. The two young men in overalls and white helmets climbed into one of the rescue boats and were rowed to shore.

Lucie watched them come, conscious of a queer inner excitement. Englishmen! She knew then how hungry she was for the sight and sound of a British face and voice. The Pasha, himself, went down to meet the pair who had landed so unceremoniously at his villa, and bid them welcome.

Lucie, standing there on the verandah, shading her eyes with one hand, experienced a definite dismay as the two figures advanced. One of them, a fair-haired boyish-looking man with a sun-browned face, had taken off his helmet and even in the distance he was vaguely familiar to her. Once he came into focus her heart gave a jolt.

Peter! Peter Callow, her old friend in the Signals, who had once been more than half in love with her and with whom she had always

162

been good friends.

She had a momentary inclination to run—she couldn't, she *mustn't* meet Peter here. He knew Crash. He would be able to tell Crash where she was. Above all things she did not want that. But it was too late for escape.

The young officer had seen and recognised that slender figure with the brown curly head and came running through the garden toward her, waving his helmet.

'Lucie! By all that's holy—Lucie!'

She surrendered then to her delight at seeing Peter and that burning desire which she knew was within her, to get news of Crash.

Holding out her hand, she said:

'It's good to see you, Peter, and the biggest surprise!'

'Much more of a surprise for me to find you here in the wilderness!' he exclaimed.

'What are you doing here?'

He pulled out a handkerchief and wiped his hot, wet face.

'Phew! We had a close shave, but Middleton landed her nicely. We were just on our way to Alex. You know I was transferred to Khartoum. Middleton's a friend of mine in the Legation at Khartoum and he asked me to fly down in his private 'plane with him to Alex for the week-end, but it looks to me as though we shall be spending it on the Nile, instead!'

Lucie said:

'You're the last person in the world I

163

expected to see to-day.'

'Same applies to you. And I suppose,' young Callow added, 'you realise that everybody in Cairo has been searching high and low for you. What in heaven's name are you doing here?'

She had no time to answer that question just then. Jack Middleton, the owner of the 'plane arrived on the scene with Ramdan Pasha and introductions were made.

Middleton was a short dapper man with dark hair and moustache. Afterwards, Lucie learned that he was one of the richest young men in the Diplomatic Corps in Egypt and one of the most astute. But he liked to give the reverse impression. At first meeting he appeared as the typical Englishman of foreign conception. Drawl, monocle and humorous laughter.

Unlike Peter Callow, he knew nothing about Lucie, and after shaking hands with her, whispered to his friend:

'I say, old chap, didn't know we were going to run up against English angel with long eye-lashes. What's she doing here?'

Peter whispered back:

'She's an old friend of mine—I'll tell you later.'

There was general excitement in the big villa that afternoon, and at five o'clock they all gathered in the beautifully cool lounge where Madame Ramdan held tea. She liked to have it served in English custom and the two young men from Khartoum found themselves regaled by a very British meal; scones, honey, home-made chocolate cake, strawberries and ice-cream.

The first opportunity that Lucie was given to speak to Peter alone was when the meal ended. Middleton went off with the Pasha's chauffeur who was a skilled mechanic, to examine the 'plane and estimate just what damage had been done. Lucie put on sun glasses and a hat, and walked out into the garden with Peter.

He took her arm and said:

'Now, my dear, I want to know everything.'

Her heart beat a trifle faster and she said:

'Well, how much do *you* know?'

'Just what was current news in Cairo when I left, which was soon after your wedding with Lorrimer. I know you vanished mysteriously after the ceremony and it's been a complete mystery ever since. I, myself, was damned upset at the time. I thought perhaps that something awful had happened to you. But I got shot up to Khartoum suddenly. You know I was to have gone back to England, but a lot of leave has been cancelled this year owing to the state of tension in Europe. In Khartoum, of course, I did get odd bits of news from friends, but merely to say that you hadn't turned up and that Lorrimer was in a bad state.'

Lucie's face flooded with colour. Those heartbeats of hers were quickening now so that

165

it was almost painful to draw breath. Being with Peter, hearing him talk about Crash, had torn from her any peace of mind that she had gained through living here in the wilderness. She was fully conscious that she was the most miserable girl on earth. She said:

'Why should he be in a bad state? He only married me because of the money . . .'

Peter Callow released her arm and looked down at her with puzzled eyes.

'What money, Lucie?'

'Then you *don't* know.'

'No, I tell you I was completely staggered when I heard you'd vanished, and I don't think anybody understands.'

'Except Crash, himself,' she said, bitterly.

'Well, what is the explanation? It's all so odd. I thought you were very much in love with Crash.'

She shut her eyes, thankful that the dark glasses hid them from Peter.

'So I—was.'

'And he was with you, or why should he have wanted to marry you?'

Lucie paused, took off her glasses and looked up at the young man for a moment.

'Listen, Peter,' she said earnestly. 'You've always been awfully nice to me and I've always appreciated your friendship. If you want to be a friend to me now, you've got to swear that you won't repeat a single word I say to you or let anybody know that I'm here. You can square your friend for me, too, can't you?'

He frowned.

'Yes, of course, but why—?'

'It's imperative to me,' she said in a low voice, 'that Crash shouldn't find me.'

'But you're his wife.'

'By law, yes, but that's as far as it goes. I left him immediately after the ceremony.'

'Well, anything you tell me is in confidence,' said Peter.

She told him, then, the whole story of Edgar Lorrimer's Will—the ugly unattractive story that Amanda Portlake had told her. And Peter Callow listened with amazement.

'It's the absolute *end!*' he said when she had finished, 'I'd never have believed anybody could be so low. You can't tell me that Crash Lorrimer really played such a cad's trick on you!'

Lucie shrugged her shoulders. There was a weariness, a complete lack of life about her that distressed young Callow greatly. Poor little Lucie! How changed she was. Pretty as ever, sweet as ever, but so crushed . . . yes, that was the word . . . it was as though all the joy of living had been crushed right out of her. And little wonder if what she had told him was true. He had never heard anything more monstrous.

'I know Crash had a reputation for "fun and games" in Cairo, but I never thought he was a mercenary blackguard,' he said.

Lucie swallowed hard.

167

'I never thought it, either, Peter. It was a pretty rude awakening for me, I can tell you.'

'But why the hell did you marry him? You must have been crazy. Why be a party to such a damned awful scheme?'

'Oh, there are a lot of reasons,' she said. 'And the first and most definite I suppose, was because I—love Crash. I loved him so much that I wanted him to be happy. If the money meant all that to him, I wanted him to have it. And in any case, the Will was unfair. Poor old Mr Lorrimer meant it for the best, but it isn't a Will that should ever have been made. Crash shouldn't have been forced into marrying me.'

'He wasn't forced into it,' said Peter Callow hotly. 'And in my opinion, no decent fellow would have gone through with it. Why, to make use of *you* knowing how much you cared about him, and knowing what a darling you are, just so that he could get the cash and then carry on with that foul woman, Amanda Portlake . . .' He broke off, shaking his head.

'It was Amanda with Crash before it was me,' said Lucie in a small voice. 'And I don't think it was ever *me* at all—it was just the money!'

Peter Callow thought hard for a moment. There were certain aspects of this story which puzzled him. After a moment he said:

'I don't quite understand why Lorrimer put up such a show of heartbreak when you left. He really needn't have gone to those lengths. I

168

heard he was searching for you in a state of lunacy. And I haven't actually heard his name connected with Amanda's since you left.'

Lucie shook her head.

'Oh, he's with Amanda all right, and if he is looking for me, it is only because his conscience worries him, I expect. Crash isn't all bad, you know. Nobody knows that better than I do. I expect he wondered if I'd thrown myself into the Nile or something. But I'm not going to get in touch with him. He might think he *ought* to live with me now and *that*, I couldn't bear.'

Peter, looking down at her, realised suddenly what this girl had suffered. What she was still suffering. There was something so fine, so brave about her. He wondered what other girl would have made such sacrifices for any man. Lucie had just eliminated herself—in order to give Crash Lorrimer his money.

'It really is monstrous!' Peter burst out, hotly.

'Well, don't forget that you've promised not to let anybody know that I'm here, and you've got to tell Jack Middleton so,' Lucie reminded him.

Ferial came running out at that moment, and hailed them:

'Mees! Mees! Let us all swim. It is not too hot now and Father will lend a swim suit for Mr Callow and his friend.'

'That sounds all right to me,' said Peter.

169

He found Lucie's hand and pressed it.

'We'll have another talk later,' he whispered. 'You know what I've always felt about you, Lucie, and I haven't changed. Anything I can do for you . . .'

'You're a dear,' she said, 'and all my thanks. It really has cheered me up seeing you again. I've been very—lonely.'

They talked again that night after dinner. It was impossible for the 'plane to be mended before morning.

The Pasha was sending up to the aerodrome at Khartoum for the new part which was necessary to put the machine into order again. But neither Jack Middleton nor Peter were much put out by their enforced change of plans. Being guests of the wealthy Egyptian in his palatial villa was better than staying at an hotel in Alexandria. He was a perfect host, and they dined and wined royally that night, and were afforded every hospitality. Ramdan Pasha was never happier than with English guests in his house.

When the big glittering stars were studding the Egyptian sky and the atmosphere was several degrees cooler, Lucie and Peter walked together in the gardens.

He spent a fruitless hour pleading with her to go back to Cairo.

'I don't think you ought to stop here, shut away like this. It's no life for you, although these Egyptians are damned nice people. But you can't be here forever, can you? And then what are you going to do with you life? It's just ruined. You're married to Lorrimer, and yet you're not. The position is impossible.'

'It would be more impossible if I went back to Cairo,' she protested. 'I repeat, I will never allow Crash to live with me just because he thinks he ought to, and if I fade out, he'll eventually forget my existence and live as he wishes to. Possibly when the Ramdans no longer want me, I shall slip quietly back to England.'

'But aren't you even going to allow Lorrimer to support you?'

'No,' she said, 'I just want to vanish out of his life.'

'I don't think old Mr Lorrimer would be very pleased at this state of affairs.'

'No, I don't suppose he would be, but he should never have made that Will.'

'Well, I don't like going off tomorrow and leaving you here like this. Now that we're back in touch, you must write to me. Let me help look after you . . . please, my dear.'

She smiled at him. There were not many smiles on Lucie's face these days, but she was genuinely grateful to the young man for his kindly interest and concern for her. She told him so.

'I will write to you, Peter, so long as I know you'll keep my confidence, and never mention my name to a soul who knows Crash or myself.'

'If that's what you wish,' he said a trifle reluctantly. 'In any case, I don't expect I'll see much more of Cairo. I shall be in Khartoum for the next year and I believe the Buckinghamshires are due to go back to England in the spring. But where will you be all this winter, Lucie?'

'With Ferial, I expect.'

'Lucie, it's no life for you . . .'

He paused, took both her hands and held them fast. She looked so small and sweet in her white evening dress, and her sun-browned arms and neck were so much too thin; her eyes so big and wistful. She roused all that was protective in the young man. And the glamour of the night in the beautiful gardens of the Egyptian villa stirred him to very vivid recollections of other evenings which he had spent with Lucie. Evenings when he had been hotly in love and hoping that he might stand a chance with her. He was only a junior subaltern and not in a position to propose to any girl, but he had thought Lucie the sweetest person he had ever met and once he had hoped that in the future she might care for him. But of course her engagement and subsequent marriage to Lorrimer had finished all that.

Now, when he knew that she did not mean to return to Lorrimer, hope revived in Peter Callow.

'Listen, Lucie darling,' he said. 'If you could get your freedom from Lorrimer, could I . . . could I . . . I mean, couldn't I do something about it? I'm hopeless at explaining myself, but you know I was always crazy about you and if you'd let me . . .'

He broke off. She looked up at him sadly. He was such a dear; good-looking, amiable, with so much to commend him. She knew girls in Cairo who were very keen about Peter Callow. Yet she could never feel that way about him. Nor about any man, except Crash. More than ever tonight, standing out here in the garden with Peter, Lucie realised how completely enslaved she was by Crash, and would be until she died.

She said:

'I do thank you so much, Peter, but my engagement and my farce of a marriage were the first and last in my life. They'll never be repeated.'

'Oh, darling,' said Peter, unhappily. 'It's all so wrong and you look so really wretched . . . it's almost more than I can bear.'

Then Lucie broke down a little. She whispered: 'It's almost more than I can bear at times, too, Peter.'

He put both arms around her, and she surrendered to the embrace. The boy stroked her hair gently and she wept her heart out there against his shoulder. He was filled with an immense indignation against Crash

Lorrimer who had done this thing to Lucie. But he could see no method of righting the wrong and his heart was sore within him.

Lucie did not join the others after that hour with Peter. As she said to him, she had made herself a sight by crying and she asked him to tell the others that she had gone off to bed.

But when she went to bed, it was not to sleep. It was to bury her face in the pillow and sob brokenheartedly, late into the night. Peter's coming here had disturbed her horribly; stirred up all the agonised craving for Crash. She wondered how she was going to go through with it.

By that next afternoon, Jack Middleton's 'plane was put in order and the two young men took their departure to Alexandria.

Lucie was quite calm when she said goodbye to Peter. In a way she was sorry to see him go. He was a link with the old life. Yet a link, perhaps, which she was better without.

'Nobody will ever know through me that you're up here, and I've squared Jack about it,' were Peter's parting words. 'If you ever want me for anything, you'll know where to find me, Lucie. The Signals Mess, Khartoum.'

After he had gone—indeed for many long days following that unexpected visit—Lucie found it hard to settle down to her work with Ferial. She found herself in a state of nervous tension that threatened to get the better of her.

And then suddenly Ferial was taken ill. The nearest doctor was in Khartoum. He was brought to the villa in the Ramdans' private aeroplane. His diagnosis of the young Egyptian girl was appendicitis, but she not was in any urgent danger. She could be easily taken to Cairo, he said, where there was a first-class surgeon, and plenty of good nurses.

Then Ramdan Pasha approached Lucie.

'I know you wish to remain hidden from your friends,' he said, 'but I beg you to come with us, if only for a few days. My little daughter loves you. Do not leave her while she is ill.'

Lucie hesitated only for a moment, then agreed to go. The Ramdans had been good to her. If the child needed her, she would not leave her. And added to this, a queer excitement rose in Lucie at the very thought that she *might* see Crash . . . or at least hear first-hand news of him.

They travelled that night by special train which the Pasha arranged to take them down to Cairo. Ferial was in some pain but not bad. Her devotion to her English companion was touching. And Lucie forgot her own troubles completely in the endeavour to make things as happy as possible for the sick girl.

The moment they reached Cairo, Ferial was conveyed by ambulance to hospital, and Lucie to the Ramdans' house in Gezira. This was a palatial residence standing in a large garden, not far from the Sporting Club.

It gave Lucie a strange shuddering feeling to be back here . . . to see that British Club . . . to remember the days which she had spent there with Crash. Gezira! Dear God! here was Olive Langham's flat . . . here she had been married . . . from here, she had run away in an agony of mind which was very little better even today. That had been in April and now it was June. Gezira was quiet. A great many Army officers would be on leave. The English and American tourists would have gone.

Where was Crash? Peter Callow had been unable to give her news of him. Possibly he had been given leave for his honeymoon. (It made Lucie shiver with pain to think of that word.) Perhaps he was in England, with Amanda somewhere close at hand. He was a married man, by law, but he would feel no responsibilities toward his wife in these circumstances. Possibly he was in the South of France . . . with Amanda!

That afternoon, Ferial was operated upon with great success; that night the Ramdans gave an enormous party to their Egyptian friends in Cairo to celebrate the fact that their beloved daughter had come through the operation, and had been spared to them.

But Lucie could not bear the festive atmosphere. She was weary of Egyptians, tarbooshes, and the loud staccato language. She longed suddenly for English people and an

English atmosphere. Something, she knew not what, drove her to enter the Continental-Savoy Hotel. Shepheard's was closed for the season. The Continental was the only hotel open during the hot weather. There, she would see people of her own race again. There, she might meet somebody who could give her news of *him.*

There were few people in the lounge. Nobody that Lucie knew. A lonely little figure, she sat down and ordered herself Turkish coffee and some cigarettes.

The manager of the hotel passed her, bowed, then walked past her again, giving her a puzzled look. Where had he seen the young English lady before? Ah! but *of course.* Excitedly he recalled the thought of the English officer, the rich Mr Lorrimer. Every day, for two months now, Mr Lorrimer had come here searching for his wife, or hoping for news of her. It was well-known in Cairo that Mrs Lorrimer had vanished soon after the wedding. And yesterday, Mr Lorrimer, looking so sad, so ill, had told the manager that his search had ended. He no longer believed that his wife was in Egypt. He even feared that she was dead. He was leaving for England at the end of this week.

But this lady, with her brown curls and her big sad eyes, this *was* Mrs Lorrimer. The manager knew her. He had known her when she was Miss Bryant, secretary of the old Mr

Lorrimer. She had often come here with friends, dining or dancing.

The manager went to the telephone-room.

'Get me the Officers' Mess of the Royal Buckinghamshires,' he said to the girl on duty, 'and ask to speak to Lieutenant Lorrimer. Say that it is the manager of the Continental-Savoy who wants him and that it is urgent . . . very, *very* urgent!'

XV

At half-past nine, Lucie finished her coffee, lit another cigarette and decided to return to the Ramdans' villa and go to bed. It had been a tiring day, what with the journey, the anxiety over Ferial and the excitement of being back in Cairo.

She rose and walked slowly through the lounge. She wore neither coat nor hat, but only a thin dark blue afternoon dress with a white turned-down collar and silky bow which made her look absurdly young. The night was hot. A real summer's night in Egypt. Lucie contemplated walking home across the Kasr-el-Nil Bridge. It would be nice to stand there awhile and watch the feluccas drift down the river in vivid moonlight. It was poignant pain, yet ecstasy, to remember that night of the felucca party when she had sat beside Crash and had believed him to be completely hers. So vividly she could remember the way his blue handsome eyes had looked at her, the way he had touched her, kissed her. The flame of passion had leapt so hotly between them, then! How could it have all been acting? How could that perfect dream of love have been just pretence on his part? Sometimes she could hardly believe it true!

Yet, bitterly she told herself that any moment she might see him enter this hotel with Amanda, sleek and lovely, laughing in her subtle, witty way, at his side.

A thick-set man wearing horn-rimmed glasses, an Englishman, strolled into the lounge. He was in dinner-jacket and smoking a cigar. Lucie recognised him at once. It was old Lorrimer's solicitor, Henry Culverton. Very many times during the old man's illness, Lucie had had to deal with Mr Culverton.

Before she could escape, the lawyer had seen and recognised that small figure in dark blue. A moment of amazement on his part and then he rushed at her.

'My *dear* Miss Bryant. I mean, Mrs Lorrimer . . .'

That last name made the blood rush to Lucie's cheeks. She tried to smile and behave with a composure which she was far from feeling.

'Good evening, Mr Culverton,' she said, formally.

'But, my dear young lady!' he exclaimed, excitedly, 'where have you come from? Where *have* you been? You don't seem to realise that we've all been searching for you for two whole months!'

She stared.

'Searching for me?'

'But of course. My *dear* young lady. Can you imagine the state of mind in which you left your husband when you disappeared on your wedding day?'

Lucie swallowed nervously.

'I don't see why. I carried out the terms of Mr Lorrimer's Will and married Crash. He did not want me. He wanted somebody else and . . .'

'See here, see here!' broke in the lawyer, protestingly. 'You've got the wrong end of the stick, my child. Now come and sit down and let us talk.'

'Surely there isn't much to say.'

'I think there is a great deal to be said so far as I can see. You have got *all* the wrong ideas.'

Lucie, feeling slightly dazed, walked with Mr Culverton to a sofa, and sat down. He looked at her quizzically over the rim of his glasses.

'Are you telling me you left young Conrad immediately after your wedding because you thought it was his wish?'

'I know that it was.'

'Who said so?'

'Amanda Portlake told me the whole story.'

'Miss Portlake! Ah! . . .' the lawyer nodded and looked at the pale ash of his cigar. 'So that's it. That's exactly what Conrad feared.'

It seemed queer to hear him call Crash by his rightful name. Lucie had never heard anybody else do it. She was conscious, too, of an inner rising excitement. So Crash had been searching for her—wanting her. That was news, indeed. Her heart was hammering, but she turned a defiant young face to Mr Culverton.

'If you want to know what I feel, I think that first of all it was an outrageous Will for Mr Lorrimer to have made; and secondly, more of an outrage that Crash should have pretended to be in love with me. I should have respected him if he had told me the truth and made it a business deal.'

'I know. There is a lot to be said on your side. Poor child! The whole thing must have been a terrible shock, but if Miss Portlake had not interfered, all would have been well. And as for young Conrad *pretending* to be in love with you—that is most unjustified. Not only was he deeply in love with you the day he married you, but he has been in a shocking state since you left. Indeed, there have been times when I have feared what he might do.'

That made Lucie draw in her breath.

'But it can't be so. He married me for the money. He wanted Amanda Portlake . . .'

181

'Nothing of the kind,' broke in the lawyer. 'He wanted you. Would you like proof of that fact? Shall I tell you that for the last two months, he has spent all his time and much of his money searching Egypt for you. Heaven alone knows where you have been hidden. You vanished as though the earth had swallowed you up.'

'I was not far from Khartoum,' she said in a low voice. 'In the villa of Ramdan Pasha.'

'Ah! Who would have thought of looking for you there?'

'I have been companion to his daughter.'

'Well, you were very mistaken in what you did, if you will forgive me saying so. Conrad has been half off his head. What is more, when I saw him yesterday, he told me that he was handing in his papers—resigning his Commission because he could no longer afford to remain in the regiment. His polo-ponies are up for sale, and at the end of this week he leaves for England.'

Lucie stared at the lawyer, her face red, then white.

'But why, why?'

'Because he says that he will not touch one penny of his father's money until he finds you. He would not accept the money under such conditions. Don't you understand, my dear young lady, that although poor Conrad behaved badly in the beginning—and he is the first to admit it—once he had come to know

182

you, he began to love you. He went to this wretched girl who is responsible for all the trouble and told her what he felt. He explained that he wished to see no more of her—to devote the rest of his life to you. What she told you was the revenge of a jealous woman. I assure you, Mrs Lorrimer, that you have done Conrad an injustice and hurt yourself for nothing.'

Lucie sat silent. It took her several minutes to credit what Henry Culverton was telling her. Could it be true? *Could it?* Had Amanda lied that night on the felucca? Was it really true that Crash had regretted his first decision and married her that day because he really loved her? After all the agony of mind through which she had passed, all the bitterness and disillusion, it seemed too much for Lucie to come back here and learn that her sacrifice had been in vain. She need not have left him! He did not want Amanda. He wanted *her.* How could she doubt that fact if he was refusing to touch the money and leaving his regiment.

She drew a long deep breath.

'Oh, Mr Culverton,' she said under her breath, 'why didn't I know all this before?'

'Why didn't you ask him what he really felt?'

'Because I was afraid he might lie again— just to keep me with him for the sake of the money. And I wanted him to have what his father left. I didn't want to be responsible for taking it from him.'

The lawyer looked at her.

'You're a very fine, very brave person, my dear,' he said gently, 'and exactly what my old friend Lorrimer always thought you were. The finest possible wife for Conrad. But I wish you had spared yourself the needless sacrifice.'

A little pulse beat in Lucie's throat. A great aching longing to see Crash was welling up inside her. The relief of knowing that he had not gone straight to Amanda, as soon as she, Lucie, left him, and that he was not leading the gay, futile, selfish life she had imagined, brought her unspeakable relief.

'Oh, Mr Culverton,' she said brokenly, 'where is Crash now?'

'In Cairo, somewhere. Possibly at the Mess or maybe out for the evening with friends. He is a great deal with his Colonel. Mrs Langham has been very kind to him.'

Lucie suddenly leaned forward and put her hands to her face. Hands that were cold and trembling, despite the heat of the night. She felt that her whole being was in a wild uproar. She could scarcely think straight. Everything that Mr Culverton had said was so contrary to the things she had been thinking about Crash all these long, lonely weeks.

And inside her heart she was crying out: 'Crash . . . *Crash* . . .'

Mr Culverton looked in the direction of the hotel entrance. A young man had just entered the lounge. A tall, graceful, familiar figure, in

184

evening clothes, bare-headed. Mr Culverton glanced quickly at Lucie. Her face was still hidden in her hands as though she was still struggling, mentally, with herself. Mr Culverton rose to his feet. He walked towards the young man who had just entered and hailed him.

'Conrad,' he said, softly.

Crash Lorrimer turned, saw his solicitor and greeted him with some surprise.

'Hullo, sir. Are you here?'

'Yes, and I have news for you, my boy.'

'I know,' said Crash, 'I know already. The manager has just 'phoned me. He saw her come in. Where is she? *Where is she?*'

Mr Culverton nodded in the direction of Lucie's bowed young figure. Crash Lorrimer took one look at it and then sprang toward Lucie. In a voice of intense, suffocating emotion, he called her name:

'*Lucie!*'

At the sound of that voice, that beloved husky voice which she had not heard for so long, Lucie's head shot up. She saw him standing there, before her. Crash, her darling, her *husband*. Crash looking handsome and excited, but oh, so much older. It gave her a shock to see the change in him. His face, dark-brown, was painfully thin. There were deep lines carved on either side of his mouth, and his eyes were not the gay and reckless eyes of the Crash with whom she had fallen in love.

185

They were serious, pain-filled eyes. The eyes of a man who has suffered.

Everything that was sheer woman in her rose to the surface and wiped out any resentment which she had ever harboured against him. He was the man she loved. That was all she remembered. The man whom she loved more than life itself, and for whom she would willingly have sacrificed that life.

'Oh Crash!' she said under her breath, 'oh, my darling, *darling!*'

The next moment she was in his arms. The lounge was deserted, but Crash Lorrimer would not have cared if it had been full. It was so marvellous to have found Lucie; to know that she was alive, to be within sight and sound of her again. It drove him temporarily crazy. He stood with her crushed in his arms, kissing her madly. And between the fevered kisses, he whispered a dozen crazy, endearing things.

'Lucie, where have you been? God, Lucie, you've punished me enough. Whatever I've done, I've paid for it. Lucie, my lovely one, my little sweet . . . God, Lucie, I love you, I love you. I've been half mad with wanting you. Lucie, where *have* you been?'

She could not answer for a few moments. Locked there in his embrace, she held fast to him, returning his kisses with complete abandonment.

She was his, completely his. She always had been. And now she knew that he was hers.

This could not be acting. There was no need for it. This was a man who had loved her and missed her as intolerably as she had missed him. And gradually the realisation crept over her that she had misjudged him, that she had been too hasty when she had run away from him that dreadful day.

His burning kisses fell upon her eyelids, her brown curls, her soft cheeks which blushed to crimson under the pressure of his lips. And when the tempest of emotion which was shaking them both to the uttermost, died down a little, Crash released her. With one arm still about her, he led her to the sofa which she had just vacated, and sat down there at her side. One of her hands was locked in his. He could feel it trembling. He could not tear his gaze from her. And he found her much as she found him . . . changed, thin—marked by suffering. He said:

'My God, darling, this is a miracle—getting you back—knowing that you don't hate me any more.'

'I've never hated you. I only resented what I thought you'd done to me. It broke my heart, Crash. It broke my heart, darling.'

'Oh, my darling, it must have done. I would have given anything to spare you that pain. I know you love me. No woman has given what you've given, nor done what you've done. When I realised that you'd married me just to give me the money, and then left me, I knew

187

how much you did care. To make such a sacrifice—for me—oh, Lucie, I didn't deserve it, darling.'

'But I didn't know the truth, Crash. I thought you wanted to get rid of me—that you wanted Amanda.'

At that name, Crash Lorrimer stiffened in every limb.

'Amanda Portlake left Egypt six weeks ago,' he said. 'I hounded her out of it. Yes, I made things so hot for her, that she had to go. And if I could have done more than that to her, I would have done it. She is responsible for all that you've been through. Oh, I don't deny that I'm responsible, too. But it was only in the beginning that I behaved so rottenly, Lucie. I fell in love with you once I got to know you. And I married you because I loved you. Everybody will tell you that. Culverton, Olive Langham—they all know what I felt about you. And what it meant to me when you disappeared.'

'I know now. I believe it now, Crash. I can *feel* it.'

'I've been half out of my mind, looking for you. Oh, my darling, where have you been?'

She told him briefly what had happened to her since that day when she had run away from the Langhams' flat. He listened without taking his blue, intent gaze from her. When she had finished, he said:

'God, if only I'd known! Just a few hundred

188

miles up the Nile. What days and nights of agony we might have saved each other, my sweet.'

Lucie was silent for a moment. She was almost exhausted by emotion. She could only sit there, holding on to his hand, returning his long ardent gaze, and asking herself whether it was a dream—whether she would wake up and find that he was gone and that she was alone, hopeless, despairing again. At last she said:

'Crash, you *are* quite sure that you do want me?'

'Do you think I want the money?' he asked abruptly. 'Hasn't old Culverton told you that I meant to give it all up anyhow, until I'd found you again.'

'Yes, he did, and, oh, I *do* believe you,' she added quickly, 'but—'

'But I don't blame you for doubting,' he said, 'after all, I behaved *rottenly* in the beginning. I've no excuse for myself. I only ask you to wipe out the memory of it, Lucie. I love you better than anything in the world, now. You *will* believe that, won't you?'

She nodded dumbly and her eyes filled with tears.

He said:

'Of course, you must leave the Ramdans at once. You say the girl is all right, so you've done your duty. I can't let you stay there another hour. I shall drive you round and speak to the Pasha, myself. I'm sure he will understand.'

'I'm sure he will,' said Lucie, 'he's been very good to me.'

He stood up and pulled her on to her feet, beside him.

'Come along, my sweet. Straight to Gezira.'

'But surely I'd better stay there tonight . . .'
He took both her hands and held them to his breast.

'Darling,' he said gently, 'have you forgotten that you're my wife? You left me on our wedding day. But now you've come back and it's still—our wedding day!'

Her whole being lit up with a flame of wild sweet happiness. She did not argue or protest. His wishes were hers, now and for always. She walked with him, hand-in-hand, out of the hotel into the starlit purple velvet of the Egyptian night.